Erimentha Parker's To Do List
By Ruby Granger

Dedicated to Mrs Probert
because I promised I would dedicate my first book to you

1

Erimentha Parker's First Day at Lady Nightingale's School
for Girls: Morning To Do List
1. *Wash face and brush teeth*
2. *Put on suncream*
3. *Do a perfect french braid*
4. *Make sure uniform is neat*
5. *Eat something nutritious for breakfast*
6. *Fill up water bottle and pack a snack for break-time*
7. *Check that all extension projects are packed*
8. *Read to calm down*

Blue-black ink glistens against crisp white paper, and I read
the list over carefully to check for mistakes. One of my bullet
points is a little bit bigger than the others, but it's not so
messy that I'll have to redo it. I pin it carefully to the cork
board above my desk and learn it by heart, staring so hard
that my eyes go fuzzy and I get an ache in my belly.

It's the third time in the last hour I've got up from my
armchair to write a list and, with a sigh, I sit back down to
my book. I'm reading *A Little Princess* for maybe the twelfth
time and can almost recite my favourite passages by heart. I

speak Sara's words aloud to my empty bedroom and imagine that I am with her in Miss Minchin's schoolhouse and have just taken her for my best friend. My cinnamon-scented candle casts a dull yellow light on the wall, the same shade of gold as when a torch is passed under the page of an old paperback. If I concentrate hard enough, I can almost pretend that I am reading under the covers after lights out.

Ever since I first read Malory Towers, I've been begging my mum to let me go to boarding school, but she says there's no way she's prepared to go so long without seeing me. And so, instead of a majestic castle on the Cornish Coast, I am going to Lady Nightingale's School for Girls — a private school twenty minutes away. I'd been on the waiting list since my ninth birthday, but a scholarship opportunity didn't open up until last year — and my parents simply couldn't afford the fees without one. There were two interviews, one with the Headmaster and one with the Head of Middle School, and I was nearly shaking with nerves for both. But the teachers were nice and it seemed like the only thing the Headteacher wanted to talk about was what was happening in the news — which was fine by me. I've been reading the news everyday since Year Four, and have been watching it since Year Three. Even though I can't always understand everything, I've learnt on the job and now understand what adults mean when they talk about *Constituencies* and *Defence Ministers* and *Council Tax*. Grown-ups never quite believe it when I pry away from the World of Children to offer my political opinion. Sometimes they ask me questions, but most of the time they dismiss it with the standard compliment that I am "intelligent beyond my years". That's also what Mrs Stafford, the Head of Middle School, said in my interview. I couldn't quite work out whether I was annoyed or gratified by the comment, but I smiled and thanked her all the same because manners are important.

3

Lady Nightingale's used to be a boarding school, way back in 1881 when there were only twenty pupils, but they stopped taking boarders at the end of the Second World War (just one of the three hundred and thirty four reasons why I wish I wasn't born in the twenty first century!) and so, even if my parents *would* let me board, I'm out of luck. There are not to be any midnight feasts and nightly sleepovers for me, it seems... I still tried my best to get in contact with some of the old boarders. But, apart from Clarice Lee, a retired journalist whose email rebounded, I couldn't find the contact information for a single school alumnae who were here in the forties. I wrote Clarice's name down in my scrapbook anyway, next to a little grainy photograph, but it doesn't really add much to my research. I only included it so that all that time looking for contact information didn't feel like a colossal waste of time. Back in April, when we first found out I'd been awarded the Year Seven Academic Scholarship, I started a scrapbook all about Lady Nightingales. I found and printed every article, photo and review which I could find online, and neatly annotated them with my fineliners so that I will be well-versed in the workings of the school. I can quote our latin motto by heart, recite the school prayer and tell you mostly everything about the school's history. If there's one thing I've learnt in my eleven years it's that you should always come prepared, especially if you're nervous. And I'm petrified for tomorrow, so preparation is essential.

"Erimentha, Nathan," Mum shouts from downstairs. "Tea's ready".

I rest my worn copy of *A Little Princess* on the stool next to my armchair and blow out the candle. Tufts of cinnamon-scented smoke waft in the last warm breath of summer and I watch it dissolve into the evening air before heading downstairs.

"How are you feeling?" Mum quizzes. "Nervous or

excited?"

"Both" I return. "I'm excited to meet everyone, but I'm nervous I'm not prepared enough. Suppose all of the other girls managed to get hold of their textbooks early and have learnt them? I don't want to be behind before we've even started!"

Mum looks at me carefully for a few seconds, flitting between my eyes with a smile on her lips. She places her hand on top of mine and her engagement ring grazes my knuckle.

"Nobody's as ready as you, Bumblebee," she says. "You've spent the summer doing extension projects and reading up on KS3 BBC bitesize. How many kids your age do you think are doing that?"

She spears a piece of broccoli with her fork and munches contentedly for a few dozen seconds.

"You've even spoken to Eleanor Graham," she continues. "A real-life pupil at Nightingale's. Even she said that you needn't worry about doing work over summer".

"But she's in Year Ten," I persist. "Things have probably changed a lot since she was my age. Mrs Luton says that Year Seven is *completely* different to Year Six and that it's a huge jump"

"Really, Erimentha, you're the most hard-working eleven-year-old I know," Mum says. "I am *positive* that you've got no reason to be worried about your academics".

I look down at my spinach and broccoli pasta, feeling marginally better. Now that I think about it, Eleanor, despite being older, did nowhere near as much work as I did this summer. The other girls in my class might very well have done more than me, but I suppose I'll just have to work extra hard if that's the case.

2

I wake up before my alarm. It's rather cold and I nestle up tight under my white cotton duvet, hugging my knees to my chest. When I turned ten, my parents said that I could exchange my wrought iron single bed for a double one — they said it was one of the perks of hitting double digits. I had refused the offer, knowing that it would be a complete waste of money. I don't seem to take up much room when I sleep; either I curl up in a ball or lay with my hands by my sides, as straight as a 2B pencil. Nathan kicked up a fuss that he had not been offered a double bed too and I had to admit that his needs *were* greater than my own because, for someone so small, he takes up a surprising amount of space. When he was little, Mum and I would sometimes peek in to watch him sleep and his arms and legs were always splayed out like the starfish you can see at the local Aquarium. I asked mum and dad if he could indeed be given a larger bed and, despite the fact that it was meant to be my special treat, they said yes.

We took a whole Sunday afternoon to choose it and Nathan jumped on nearly every double bed in the store. I said sorry to the shop assistants on his behalf, knowing that they would have to straighten the sprawled bedsheets as soon as we left. He eventually decided on a deep blue bed frame with a curved headboard and it was delivered to the house four days later (though the way Nathan carried on, you would have though it had been four weeks!). Tucked away in the van, the delivery men also brought out a large cardboard box which, as luck would have it, turned out to be a filing cabinet. My parents had ordered it for me as a surprise and I spent a pleasant afternoon decanting all of my old school work (kept neatly in lever arch files) into the sleek sliding drawers. Nathan and I each felt that we had got the better deal.

My alarm clock sounds and I am out of bed within seconds. My school uniform sits neatly on my armchair, the shirt collar uncreased and the skirt's pleats meticulous. I get changed more slowly that usual, making sure that my shirt is tucked in, my skirt is exactly one inch below my kneecap and my knee-high green socks are even.

I open the curtains to let in the bleak autumn light and it streams across my made bed, highlighting the few creases on the bedspread. I close my eyes to the morning and say a mental hello to the large oak tree just outside my window. It's close enough that I could climb out if I wanted to (not that I ever would). The leaves, still a vibrant green, quiver in the new autumn breeze and I ease open the top window panel to let in some fresh air. Wispy strands of hair wave about my face and I take in three deep breaths, the ones that they teach you in yoga classes. The air is sweet and clean and I gaze absentmindedly at the forest across from the house. The trees waver in the cold September air and I watch a muntjac stroll across the thickets of tree roots. Its spindly legs crunch against the permanent leaf litter and it leans down to sniff a something. The fur of its chestnut coat sticks up slightly, as though it too has just woken up from a long slumber, and I watch until the deer stumbles out of sight.

It embarrasses me that I have such a large wardrobe, especially since only the right wall is actually used for clothes: my dresses, pleated skirts and jumpers are hung up in neat rows, with shoes, pyjamas and underwear in the drawers underneath. The whole left side of the little room stores stationery and I have made the back wall into a dressing table of sorts. Since learning about the Victorians last year, I have kept a washbasin on top of the table — the jug was Grandmama's and is embellished with reams of roses twirling up the side of the china. I always make sure its filled with clean water so that I can pretend every morning that I was born in the nineteenth Century. Having dabbed my cheeks dry with a flannel, I pull my hair tightly into a braid and secure it with a large, green bow (which I have already checked is school regulation) before smiling once in the mirror.

I am booked onto the school coach service but Nathan doesn't start school until next Tuesday and so Mum has agreed to drive me in for the first three days. It's cold and the windows steam up with body heat when we climb in. My backpack is heavy with pencil cases, post-it notes and books and I check its contents against my list as we pull out. On the literature front, I've brought a Robert Frost poetry anthology, Malory Towers and a biography of Florence Nightingale which I found in the local library (she's one of my greatest inspirations, after J.K Rowling, Barack Obama and Queen Elizabeth I, and I want to learn as much as I can about her now that I'm attending a school named after her!). I've also left room for the books I'm planning to take out from the school library. On the tour last May, I passed by several which looked particularly good and made note of them on my sticky-note pad so I'd remember to take them out on my first day. I still have the note and have stuck it at the front of my blackbird notepad alongside fourteen other important reminders for the day. I like to keep one notebook dedicated solely for my post-it notes and I bring it with me everywhere I go. It's officially known as 'The Book of Reminders' and it makes sure that I don't lose or forget anything important. I've already lined a page in blank sticky notes, ready to jot down any new friends' email and home addresses.

The car is silent (which, I've got to admit, is pretty unusual!) and so mum has switched the radio to Classic FM, and Bach's third piano concerto drifts pleasantly through the heated car, the optimistic chords blending with the outside drizzle. I watch the raindrops dance across the glass, joining with their companions to form large, magnificent water droplets. Outside, the starved fields drink in the rain thankfully. The last few weeks were really dry, and the grass became parched with sunshine. We pass by several dog walkers wearing their macintoshes for the first time in months, their dogs trotting along, nonplussed by the weather.

"Awful weather," Mum says, adhering to the British, weather-complaining stereotype.

On the contrary, I am rather enjoying the bright and even temperament. I love the rain.

"Do you want me to come in with you?" Mum asks, turning from the wheel for a second so as to make eye-contact.

"No, I should be fine," I assure her. "I learnt the school map over the holidays and think I know where everything is. Plus, I can remember seeing the office on the tour".

Mum looks a bit dismayed and I smile warmly at her.

"Anyway, Nathan's got a doctor's appointment and neither of us wants for him to be late."

"What would I do without you, Bumblebee?" she says with a laugh, patting me on the shoulder.

I'm the first new girl at the office and the receptionist smiles warmly in greeting, asking me my name and year group.

"I'm Erimentha Parker," I say confidently, taking her hand in a firm handshake. "I'm starting in Year Seven."

"Of course, Erimentha," she says bemused. "How lovely to meet you. I received your emails over the break and am happy to see that we're receiving such an organised student".

I had contacted the school with a few uniform and equipment queries, and also asked for my timetable in advance. It seemed impractical to bring in history books if I weren't even to have history on my first day.

"Are you excited?" the lady asks kindly.

"Oh yes! Very much so. I've been talking with Eleanor Graham in Year Ten about what to expect and, from what I've heard and seen, the school is simply marvellous."

The lady blushes very slightly, clearly not used to such enthusiastic pupils.

"Well, I hope that you enjoy your time here," she says as a little girl and her mother slip through the office door.

The girl is pretty in a plain sort of way. Her hair is a deep brown, so dark that it is almost black, and her fringe is perfectly trimmed in a straight line above her eyebrows. She only looks about seven.

"I just need to hand in some medicine to the nurse," the girl's mother says loudly, distracted by an incoming text message. "Can you tell her that we're here?"

The woman ignores me entirely but the little girl looks at me thoughtfully and I smile back, hoping that her medicine is for nothing serious. She looks healthy enough so I suppose she is recovering from a sports injury or minor operation of some kind. When I was around her age, I badly sprained my ankle playing tennis and had to take ibuprofen for days afterwards.

10

The receptionist leads the girl and her mother out of the room, leaving me on my own, and I take *The Collected works of Robert Frost* from my satchel while I wait, getting lost in images of 'benighted snow' and 'dimpled spiders'. When I next look up the receptionist has returned and there are seventeen other new girls crowding the office. I've made up my mind that I want to meet every girl in the year by the end of the day and so, even though I'm reluctant to put down Frost, I know that now is the best time to start.

"Hello, I'm Erimentha Parker," I say to a redhead standing nearby. "Are you starting in Year Seven too?"

The girl looks up from what I suppose to be a very thorough examination of the plywood floorboards. She seems surprised that I have spoken — the other new girls are standing in silence.

"Yeah. I'm Simone Randolph," the girl says in a strong American accent, brushing her hair behind her ears.

"Which school do you come from, Simone?" I ask, knowing that addressing people by their first names usually makes them feel more comfortable.

Sure enough, the girl gives me a genuine smile and explains that she and her parents only just moved over from Arizona.

"I'm still not used to the cold weather — it's only September and I'm already wearing thermals!" she laughs.

"I've got to admit that it's chilly this morning," I say, "but at least the last few weeks have been warm. I don't think I wore tights once over the whole of August!"

"Not me, I've been wearing my warmest sweaters and jeans," she giggles. "I can tell you, my new neighbours have sure been giving me funny looks".

"Especially since all of the other children were probably using their paddling pools every—," I fall silent as Mrs Stafford enters the office. Her shoes are just as sensible as they were last May: brown penny loafers not too different from the ones I am wearing myself. They say that you can understand a lot about a person by the shoes they wear, and from her practical and plain footwear, I predict that she is a no-nonsense kind of teacher (the best kind in my opinion).

"Welcome to Lady Nightingale's School," she says. "My name is Mrs Stafford and, for those of you who don't already know, I am the Head of Middle School. I can imagine that you're all nervous, but I hope that you're also excited. Going into senior school is of course a change, even for those pupils who were here in the preparatory department, but I am confident that, by the end of the week, you will have settled happily into Year Seven life. I have with me the three form tutors for this academic year: Miss Lacey, Mr Aldridge and Mrs Norcop. Listen carefully for your name and then please go and stand with the your form tutor".

Mr Aldridge is a History Teacher with glasses, dark hair and very slight stubble, and he leads us straight to his classroom after our names have been read out. Snaking around the upper-skirting is a massive timeline, stretching from 4000 BCE all the way to the present day. It's an excellent idea but the photographs are computer generated and pixelated and it was probably done in a rush. I take my sticky note pad from my pocket and write myself a reminder to make him a new, handmade one. The rest of the room is plastered with his students' work and so I expect he'll appreciate my efforts. There are only fourteen other girls in my class, less than half the number in my Year Six class, and I know that it is going to be easy to learn everybody's names. Mr Aldridge helps us to push the tables to the side of the room and we make a circle. It feels strangely familiar because we'd have circle time with Mrs Luton every Monday morning. I put my satchel safely to the side and take a seat next to my new teacher, with a tall, athletic-looking girl on my left.

"Alright kids. Eight of you are new this year and so we've got a lot of unfamiliar faces in this classroom. Just so that we can get to know each other a little better, we're going to go around, introduce ourselves and tell everyone our favourite thing that we did over the summer. I'll go first. I'm Mr Aldridge and, as you already know, I'll be your form tutor this year. Over the holidays my wife and I visited Cambodia and the highlight of the trip had to be visiting a local marketplace called Phsar Chas".

I stare at him in awe as the student to his left speaks about her own summer excursions — Mr Aldridge is clearly very cultural and I surely have a lot to learn from him. I quickly jot *Cambodia* down on a sticky note so I don't forget to ask him more about his travels. I miss the name of the first girl, but remember the others. Lastly, after the tall girl has introduced herself as June, my teacher motions for me to start talking. I've been mentally preparing what I am going to say and my voice rings clear over the history classroom.

"Hello, I'm Erimentha," I say cheerfully. "The best thing that I did over the summer holidays has to have been my trip to the British Library in London. It was fascinating to see the original manuscripts of my favourite books. I was particularly struck by the Moutier-Grandval Bible because the illustrations were just stunning. Did you know that, before the publication of King James I's Bible in 1611, nearly all Bibles were illustrated so that the public could understand the material?"

"Yes, I did know that, Erimentha," Mr Aldridge says, and I find myself getting a little hot. "And I agree that it is fascinating. Did you manage to find anything out about the Moutier-Grandval Bible specifically?"

"Oh yes," I say. "There wasn't much information in the library itself but I did some research when I got home and wrote a short essay on my findings. You're welcome to read it if you would like?"

Mr Aldridge assures me that that would be lovely and I notice that a dark-haired girl, Kimberly, sitting opposite from me is rolling her eyes. She has a dainty ski-slope nose and is tanned from her trip to Cancún over the summer. She looks straight at me and, whilst I may be mistaken, I seem to detect a certain malice in her pale blue irises. I try a smile and, although she returns it, her eyes remain cold. Even when I turn my attention back to Mr Aldridge, I can feel them boring into the back of my neck like UV sun rays on unprotected skin.

"Year Seven is infamous for its friendship troubles but I'm hoping that you girls will defy this stereotype and that we can all get on well this year".

The dark-haired girl whispers something to her friend and the two giggle.

"Mrs Stafford has sent me a short powerpoint to go through with you which just outlines a few of the friendship problems that you may encounter this year, as well as the ways you can resolve them".

The presentation includes those tips which I have have already read about in friendship self-help books, but I suppose that they are still useful reminders: join clubs, be yourself, tell a parent or teacher if you are finding things difficult. A fake scenario pops up on the board — two friends, Anna and Bailey, have had an argument and each is convinced that they are in the right. There is a clipart sketch of two girls in cliche pink dresses, the skirt lengths of which would certainly not meet school uniform regulations. Mr Aldridge's phone rings and he apologises profusely as he leaves the room to take it: his sister is in hospital, he explains.

Once he's gone, the classroom erupts into chatter.

"Look at how short Bailey's dress is," Izzy, the dark-haired girl's friend, exclaims, laughing.

"Oh yes!" I say, trying to erase the tensions from earlier. "Both of their skirts are frightfully short!"

"No," Kimberly corrects coldly, "Anna's dress is too *long*; it's only like four inches above her knee. I've heard that wearing your skirt that long is social suicide".

A few of my classmates look uncomfortable, their own skirts being longer than that. She notices and forces an encouraging smile.

"I didn't mean it like that — your skirts are all fine," she says kindly and my peers relax visibly in their seats.

"It's only when you wear your skirt an inch *below* the knee," she says cooly, her eyes glued to mine.

3

We stay in our forms until fifth period and so miss English, dance and French. It's a shame because I've got a stack of book reviews in my satchel that I was hoping to show my new English teacher. Nonetheless, I am excited when Mr Aldridge walks us to our Geography lesson at 1150 hours. I think I would have been able to get their quite well by myself but I expect that he doesn't want any of us getting lost on our first day. My peers chatter excitedly and I strike up conversation with June who seems lovely even though she's rather shy. We decide to sit next to one each other and I choose us two places at the same table as Kimberly and her friend. June looks at me quizzically, asking whether this is really such a good idea, but I need to get on the right side of Kimberly. I don't want to make an enemy on the first day and taking this seat shows that I am not holding any grudges. The two girls are deep in conversation and don't seem to notice that we've sat down opposite them. I unpack my satchel, taking out my two pencil cases, a pack of sticky notes, some A4 lined paper, my summer extension projects and my brand new school planner. I organise it into a neat pile on my desk, leaving enough room so that I can comfortably write.

"You're so organised, Erimentha," June laughs. "I've really

only brought a couple of pencils with me for today".

Izzy looks at me and starts giggling.

"That's probably all we'll end up needing but I like to be extra prepared." I say, looking between June and Izzy with a smile.

"Alright girls, that's enough talking please," the teacher says crisply. "For those of you that do not know, I am Miss Solomon and will be taking you for Geography this year. In primary school, silliness may have been permitted but I expect for each of you to be conscientious and sensible now that you are in Year Seven".

The two girls opposite from me are nearly in hysterics now and I give them a stern look but this only makes them laugh harder.

"Most of you seem to have mastered the act of listening, but this table," she motions to where we are sitting, "is clearly finding this to be a difficult task. Stand up please, girls and tell me your names".

I stand up so rapidly that I clunk my knee on the desk, "My name's Erimentha Parker, Miss Solomon, and I would like to apologise on behalf of our table for our behaviour," I say loudly, my heart beating with nerves.

"That's quite alright, Erimentha," Miss Solomon says, "but it was the attitude of your companions which I found to be particularly rude".

They stop laughing and Izzy even looks a little scared.

"S-sorry Miss Solomon," she says quickly.

"What possibly could have been so funny?" she asks briskly. "Share it with the class now, girls".

"We were just laughing at a joke that Erimentha told us," Kimberly says carefully.

"I see," Miss Solomon says, giving me a disapproving look.

I haven't got told off since I was about five and am distraught that I have made a bad first impression. I want to jump to my defence but I also know that it will be taken as talking back, and also as tattling, so I just sit up straighter to listen.

"We're going to start by making a mind map on the whiteboard," she continues. "I'd like for us to go around the classroom and each say just one thing to do with Geography".

My peers are coming out with fairly general words — things like 'weather', 'the environment' and 'rivers' — and so, whilst I had initially decided to comment on the sustainable city of Curitiba, I come out with 'globalisation'.

Miss Solomon falters for a second after I have spoken, "Globalisation? Erimentha, do you know what that is?"

"Well, yes. I was reading about it just the other night actually in the *Encyclopaedia Britannica*," I answer. "Globalisation is the integration of companies, businesses and cultures across the world and really is responsible for the growing global economy today. Did you know that since 1990, globalisation has allowed three hundred *million* people in China to have overcome the poverty line?"

Miss Solomon remains silent and so I continue.

"But it's not all good. Companies only really move factory locations so that they can escape from the Red Tape in this country. Do you remember in 2013 when the Bangladesh factory collapsed and killed 1100 people?" I say, looking around the classroom. "Well, that's because there weren't any real factory regulations in Dhaka. So even though globalisation can be a good thing, it has also had a really negative impact".

Kimberly and Izzy are whispering to one another but Miss Solomon doesn't seem to have noticed.

"Well, I've got to say that that was rather impressive, Erimentha," Miss Solomon says slowly. "You can have a housepoint for that excellent answer".

She dutifully puts 'globalisation' on the board and then turns to Izzy who says, 'oceans' and Kimberley who, deciding not to take the exercise seriously, says 'green'.

"And why might that be?" Miss Solomon asks with an eyebrow raised.

"Because, well it's the colour of every Geography exercise book I've ever been given," she says, as though it's the most obvious thing in the world. Our teacher doesn't say anything and reluctantly writes it on the board.

Whilst her back is turned, Kimberly leans in towards Izzy and says, just loud enough that I can hear, "Plus, it's the colour I turn when I realise I'm going to have to sit across from Little Miss I-Know-Everything for the rest of the year".

***

I ignore Kimberly for the rest of class. Nathan always calls me a Know-It-All so it's nothing new but her malice makes it hard to take as a joke. When the bell rings, her and Izzy are the first ones out of the door, determined to get to lunch quickly.

"I just want to give something to Miss Solomon quickly," I tell June. "I won't be a second".

"Okay, I'll save you a place in the queue".

Our teacher is busy with some papers and so I wait politely beside her desk. It's much tidier than Mrs Luton's was and I am especially admiring of her in and out-tray. Through the white mesh of metal, I can see that the in-tray has already accumulated a small stack of sheets, despite the fact that term only started this morning.

"Have you always loved Geography, Erimentha?" she asks.

Now that I am standing next to her, I can see just how tall she really is and I have to look up to make eye-contact.

"Well it informs everything we do and so it is surely one of the most important things that we can learn about".

She gives me a warm and genuine smile, her eyes sifting between mine. A small crease has appeared between her eyebrows, as though she is concentrating very hard on something — I know because I have this look on my face in a lot of our family photographs. There is one particularly amusing one from when I was seven and visited the Grand Canyon. We asked a fellow-tourist to snap a picture of us in front of the valley, but instead of saying 'cheese' as I had been asked to, I had been thinking very hard about how such a tremendous depression even came to be. That year, I had gone through an astronomy phase and had supposed that a giant asteroid had collided with the earth. In the photograph, I am considering this hypothesis and you can see my brain working. Grandmama thought it was so amusing that she got it framed for the mantlepiece.

"I actually wanted to give you something, Miss Solomon," I say. "You see, over the summer, I became particularly interested in hurricanes and made a booklet about everything that I found out. I thought maybe you'd like to have a look".

I hold out the sixteen-page, hand-illustrated booklet with pride and she takes it from me gently.

"Oh how lovely, Erimentha," she says, flicking through the pages with care. "Do you mind if I could keep this to have a closer look? I promise that I won't let anything bad happen to it".

She reaches a diagram which took me a particularly long time to draw — I tracked the pathway of Hurricane Katrina, documenting the appropriate air pressure and damage between 1700 and 0500 hours. I had been so proud of the illustration that I'd photocopied it to give to Juliet.

"Perhaps you could even give a short presentation to the class about what you learnt?" she suggests. "I'm sure they'd find it interesting. I'd also like to give you two housepoints, if you could take out your planner for me: one for this, and another for your excellent answer in class".

I sleekly extract the book from my satchel and turn it to the appropriate page for her to sign. She takes a fountain pen from her shirt's pocket protector, which is just like the ones that businessmen wear in the movies, and signs the page elegantly. Her handwriting is embellished with majestic loops, but not so much so that it is superfluous. I wonder whether she ever had calligraphy classes. I've watched videos on how to write that way myself but haven't yet got the hang of it — it takes me far too long for it to be practically used as my everyday handwriting and I only wish it came more naturally to me.

"Thank you, Miss Solomon," I say, "and of course I'd be delighted to give a short presentation".

I leave the classroom with a wave and set off for the lunch hall.

***

Most of my year has already gone in by the time I arrive, June included, and so I wait in line by myself. I am tempted to introduce myself to the Year Eight girls in front but they seem heavily wrapt up in their conversation and I am sure that they do not want me interrupting. Instead I take my sticky notes from my blazer pocket and brainstorm some ideas for my Geography presentation next week:

Ideas for Erimentha Parker's Hurricane Presentation:
1. *Make a powerpoint as a visual aid*
2. *Conduct a practical experiment in the classroom (find one on academia.com)*
3. *Read out my short story about the social effects of Hurricane Katrina*

* * *

"Hey, Erimentha," Someone says and I look up to see Simone, "I thought I was going to have to eat lunch by myself so it's a relief to see you".

"Yes, I was hoping to see you at break actually. Have you had a good day so far?" I ask, "We had Geography just before lunch and Miss Solomon, our teacher, is just incredible".

"That's good," My friend says, "Geography was always my favourite subject in elementary school. In third grade — year four, I mean — we made model volcanoes and erupted them in class with baking soda and vinegar".

"Oh, I've always wanted to do that experiment," I say. It's one of the top Science Fair Project ideas when you search online and it's been on my 'Potential Extension Project' list for nearly three months. "I know you've already done it once but maybe you could come over this Saturday and the two of us could make a volcano together?"

"I'd love to!" she says, "I mean, I'll have to check with my Mum but I'm sure she'll say yes. Do you want to take her mobile number?".

I peel off the top post-it note where I had previously been brainstorming, stick it to the back of The Book of Reminders then hand Simone the blank pad and a pen. She's left-handed and the newly formed words of the Parker smudge as she writes, staining both the yellow paper and her hand with blue-black streaks. Her face is framed in frizzy red strands which have escaped from her ponytail but she still manages to look smart, most likely because her uniform is as immaculate as mine — really the only difference is that she, still adapting to the cold British weather, is wearing thick woollen tights. Oh, and her skirt sits an inch above the knee, rather than an inch below but that's only because she's a few inches taller than me. We reach the front of the queue and Simone quickly passes the sticky pad over to me so that she can order. The school is serving something particularly unhealthy as a first-day-of-school treat and she happily orders the fishcake and chips. I however, being vegan, just ask for a jacket potato and then head over to the salad bar to choose some accompanying vegetables — beetroot, tomato, cucumber, sweetcorn and avocado — as well as a mixed bean salad as my source of protein. Simone similarly heaps her plate with lettuce leaves after I stress the importance of getting your Seven a Day and I cannot help but laugh at the extravagant hill of greenery which has hidden her chips. I notice June and a few girls from Mrs Norcop's form sitting at a table in the corner and she smiles when we join her.

"Hi Erimentha," June says, "And who's this, sorry?".

"Oh, this is Simone," I say, noticing my friend looking rather shy, "She's new as well".

"I used to live in Phoenix. That's why I'm wearing tights, if you're wondering," she adds, looking down self-consciously at the others' bare legs.

"I dare say that we'll all be wearing tights in a couple of weeks," I say reassuringly, "BBC weather predicts that we're going to have the coldest October on record".

Simone and I break off from the other three and start a conversation of our own, discussing the meteorological differences between England and Arizona and, later, our summer excursions. Her family arrived in Cornwall in late July and so she spent the entirety of August at home, her parents too busy unpacking furniture to take her anywhere. Her mother told her to introduce herself to the neighbours but, as I have already noticed, she is timid around new people and so I'm not surprised that she rejected this suggestion. Instead she confined herself to the house, organising her new room and then, once this was done, doing little more than watching television and painting.

"But it's not all bad," she assures me, "I do enjoy art and I managed to fill up a whole sketch book with drawings".

"You should show me some time," I suggest, "I've never been particularly artistic myself".

"What are you talking about?" June interrupts, "That diagram of a frog that you did in Geography today was excellent!"

I shake my head with a laugh. I'm frequently commended for my beautiful diagrams and project illustrations but do not accredit this to artistic ability. I'm just neat and careful. The only reason that my Cuban Tree Frog looked impressive is because I am a rather skilled copyist. There was a picture in the textbook and it wasn't too tricky to transfer it to my notes. My drawings are particularly good when I have some tracing paper on hand!

"You should have seen my drawing of the frog," June exclaims to Simone, "It was awful. I think Miss Solomon was trying not to laugh when she saw it".

"It wasn't *that* bad June," I say, "You know what, I'm just going to go and fill up the water jug. It's nearly empty and it really is so important that we stay hydrated. Did you know that 75% of Americans are chronically dehydrated?".

There are two large water machines, one on either side of the dining hall, and I notice that Izzy is filling up her jug at the one to the left. Perhaps, without Kimberley there, I will be able to secure some sort of acquaintanceship.

"Hello Izzy," I say, "How did you like Geography today?".

"Yeah, it was great," she says loudly, "I especially loved your speech about globalisation".

She turns from the water machine and looks me in the face, "Very inspiring," she says with forced gaiety.

"Next time you should teach us about monsoons," she says, "I've always wanted to learn more about those".

Before I can say anything, Izzy trips forwards and her full jug spills water all down my front. My cotton shirt sticks to the vest beneath, as though a ganon of marine leeches have latched onto my chest. The polyester of my blazer means that the water runs smoothly over the material and onto the ground, like dribble or the trail of a snail.

"Izzy," I say sternly, "What did you do that for? That was completely and utterly uncalled for".

"Sorry Erimentha, it was an accident," she shrugs and heads back to her table. Her whole expedition to the water machine was a colossal waste of time because she didn't even bring back the water, but her friends still meet her with high fives when she sits down. I, on the other hand, dutifully fill up the water jug. The Book of Reminders in my pocket is damp and I flick through the pages to survey the damage. Collectively, the notes at the front have formed an ocean of washable ink but most of the words are still legible. The only one which is unsalvageable is 'Erimentha Parker's List of the Best Pencil Brands' which was stuck on the front cover.

I set the water jug down at my table and, despite not having finished, pick up my tray to leave.

"As you can see, there was a bit of a mishap at the water machine," I explain as they examine my sopping wet shirt, "I'm going to go and get something dry on because it's really rather uncomfortable and will be even more so if it dries".

"Do you want us to meet you anywhere?" asks Simone.

"No, that's okay. I wanted to quickly visit the library anyway," I say.

***

Thankfully, I brought in a spare uniform. I've got multiples of everything, save the blazer which was too expensive to get two of. Dad insisted that my spare change would never come in useful — after all, I brought in an extra change of uniform everyday in Year Six and not once did I make use of it. I am thankful now that I didn't listen to him. I don't know how I would have been able to concentrate in the last three periods if I had had to wear damp clothing. Not only this, but I expect Mr Aldridge would have made me explain exactly what happened and telling on Izzy would make her even more resentful than she already is. I collect my Foyles Carrier Bag from the form room and get changed in an empty toilet cubicle. The shirt sleeves get stuck on my shoulders and I have to peel off the cotton, quite in the same way as when you peel a sticky note from a bad-quality pad. I stash the damp clothing into the empty carrier bag, folding the shirt as best as I can. It resembles a ball of paper, regardless.

In the bathroom mirror, I redo my french braid, my hands aching slightly as I hold them over head. I meet the eye of my reflection, our green irises swimming in the glass, and plant a smile on my face. I needn't be dismayed, I reason. Things like this happen in Senior School. Most of the parenting books that I've read say that it's a part and parcel of growing up. There will always be a little spitefulness along the way.

***

A few girls are talking in the classroom when I enter, Izzy and Kimberly amongst them, but they fall silent when they see me.

"How come you're dry?" Beth, a girl from my form, asks bluntly.

"Oh, I always bring in a spare change of uniform," I explain, "You know, for accidents like this. I want you to know, Izzy, that I don't hold any hard feelings for what happened at lunch — I know that you didn't mean to spill the water".

"Maybe not on your part," Beth snorts, "I'm still annoyed that a perfectly good jug of water was wasted on you".

26

I inhale sharply, "In my defence, I didn't exactly want to get drenched in water!".

"Well it was your own fault," Izzy says, "I mean, you were the one who tried to trip me up in the first place".

"But I never—," I start to say but Kimberly interrupts me.

"There's no point denying it, Erimentha, I saw everything from where I was sitting. Izzy was innocently filling up the water jug and when she turned around you pushed her. I don't know which school you used to go to but at Lady Nightingale's, violence is looked down upon. We've had to tell June what happened — I mean, she doesn't want to go making friends with a psychopath".

"I'm not a psychopath," I say, nearly in tears, "Even if I had deliberately spilt the water, which I didn't, I don't have the other symptoms that the DSM says are essential for a diagnosis. You are required to be irresponsible, impulsive, badly-behaved and a pathological liar and I am quite clearly none of these things!".

"Well, actually," Kimberly says, "You are a liar because you're lying about not pushing Izzy when I *saw* you do it".

"Kimberly, I really think that you are mistaken. No matter what you think you saw, I can assure you that I didn't push Izzy. I wouldn't *want* to push Izzy".

"We weren't gonna tell the rest of the form what happened at lunch but you lying has changed my mind," Beth says, "Don't you agree, guys?".

My breathing shallows. I might be able to convince June that they are lying but the form is clearly going to listen to Kimberly over me. She's the kind of girl that the parenting books highlight as 'Queen Bee material', a term coined by Rosalind Wiseman in her novel *Queen Bees and Wannabes* (possibly the best self-help book that I have read on the matter). The girls seem to be waiting for me to say something but I really don't want any more trouble and I can feel a tear on my cheek. I hang up my Foyles carrier bag on my peg and leave the classroom, only wiping it away when they can no longer see me, annoyed at my weakness. Just before the door closes behind me, I hear Kimberley's honey-roasted voice:

"I would feel bad that she won't have any friends but that's not exactly true. I mean, she's got Miss Solomon".

4

It's nearing the end of lunch and the library is practically empty. I notice that the little girl from this morning is sitting by herself on one of the purple armchairs, reading a novel embellished with strokes of lilac glitter. I never went through that phase — the 'pink spinner books', as my local librarian calls them. I suppose I find greater solace in older fiction — anything published before 1960 will likely appeal to me. Over the summer, I discovered Sylvia Plath and read 'The Bell Jar', her complete poems and also her letters to Ted Hughes. It was melancholy work, I've got to admit, but there was something undeniably valiant in her ability to transfer such dark and distressing thoughts to paper. Not only this but goodness was the imagery beautiful! I filled a whole A6 notebook with "pregnant moons" and "moonly mind somersaults": lists of quotes, photocopies of pages and annotated print-outs of poems. They don't offer psychology in Year Seven but I still made the GCSE teacher a pamphlet about the changes in mental health care, from Plath's time in McLean Hospital up until the present day. The historical element means that I can also show Mr Aldridge — I expect that he'd find that interesting.

I take out The Book of Reminders, which has been warmed

underneath the toilet hand driers. The pages are dry but crisp and they crackle like the Gryffindor Common Room fireplace as I leaf through. The list I am looking for has not been smudged at all:

Books to Take out at Lady Nightingale's
- *The Weather Handbook by Alan Watts*
- *The Definitive Book of Body Language by Allan and Barbara Pease*
- *Mansfield Park by Jane Austen*
- *The Elegant Universe by Brian Green*

With the assistance of the trusted Dewey Decimal System it only takes me a few minutes to find all four novels but, to my dismay, I find that lower school girls are only permitted to borrow two books at any given time. I reluctantly put *The Weather Handbook* and *Mansfield Park* back and take out the other two.

"These are quite tricky books," the librarian, Ms Athena, says, "Are you sure they're at the right level for you?".

"Yes, I think so," I assure her, "Green's book looks rather similar to Hawking's *A Brief History of Time* which I read and loved".

"In which case, do let me know how you get on with it," she says bemusedly, "And what was your name, lovely? I didn't catch it".

"Oh yes, sorry. I'm Erimentha Parker. Today's my first day".

"Oh well, I hope that you're settling in well and that you'll become a familiar face in the library," she says and I nod in agreement.

The bell rings and Ms Athena waves me goodbye so that she can hurry the other girls along to registration.

My classroom is nearly completely full when I enter. Mr

Aldridge must have continued with circle time in his lesson before lunch because the tables are still pushed to the sides. A few girls are scattered across the floor but most are leaning against tables. Izzy has one hand on her shoulder, complaining that it is aching and a few girls are crowding round her, asking if she's okay.

"It's just annoying because it's my *right* shoulder," she sighs, "I don't think I will be able to write this afternoon in R.S".

She whispers something else and the girls all look round at me, scowling. Ignoring them, I start reading *The Elegant Universe*, figuring that astrophysics, if anything, will be able to restore my sense of calm. Indeed, by the time Mr Aldridge greets us with 'Good Afternoon' I am heavily absorbed and tearing myself away is as difficult as it would be to tear a page out of the book itself.

"Alright kids," he says, "Can you help me put the tables back. I'd like to assign you each a desk before assembly since we didn't get a chance before lunch".

The clunking of chairs, rumble of feet and scraping of metal table legs against carpet ensues and within minutes the desks are arranged in neat rows — I check to make sure that they are parallel. Mr Aldridge says that we can sit where we like and people rush to sit with their friends, noise levels rising as they try to get someone's attention.

"Hey Erimentha," Someone shouts from the other side of the room, "Over here!".

Assuming it's June, I dodge past anarchistic Year Seven girls to reach the front of the room, but instead see Beth.

"I thought you'd like this one," she says, motioning to a single desk directly in front of Mr Aldridge's. I know that she intends for it to be unkind but I'm actually thrilled — sitting so close to the teacher will mean that we can converse about Cambodia and mental health care whilst my peers chatter

31

seamlessly about lip gloss, social media and pop music. The desk is a little bit sticky, as though fruit juice had been spilt on the surface before the holidays, and so I quickly wipe it down with a baby wipe before sitting down.

"Don't get too comfortable kids," Says Mr Aldridge, "We actually need to head over to assembly now. Be quick. We don't want to be late.".

I stand abruptly and follow my teacher out of the door, hurrying to catch him up.

"Mr Aldridge, I just wanted to check that you've registered us," I say.

I don't mean to sound rude in the slightest but I know how vital it is that he does it. Not only would he probably get into trouble with administration staff but if there were a fire, one of us could be getting burnt alive in the building, popularly thought to be the most painful way of dying, and nobody would even think to come looking for us.

"Don't worry Erimentha," he says, "I counted, and everybody's here. I signed you all in whilst you were putting back the tables and chairs".

I breathe out a smile and thank him. I want to ask him about his summer but Melody taps him on the back to ask him something about the coach drop off system. I hang behind slightly so that it will not look as though I am eavesdropping.

"Oh Erimentha, you poor thing," I hear Kimberley say with mock concern, and I turn around to meet her pale blue eyes.

"And why would that be?" I ask calmly.

"Well, firstly you were sitting alone in form and now you're walking all by yourself — even Mr Aldridge doesn't want to talk with you," she pouts.

"Aw, it always upsets me to see people who don't have any friends," Beth says to Kimberley.

I turn my back on them and continue walking but can still

hear their conversation and even when I try to unravel myself from this word-woven fishnet, their voices refract from the narrow corridor walls.

"I always wondered why some people were just friendless," Izzy says, "I mean, at my old school there were a few kids who hung out by themselves and I kind of felt bad for them. I didn't play with them because my friends didn't want to but I never really understood *why*. It's only after meeting Little Miss Pick-Me Parker that it *finally* all makes sense".

"Totally," Kimberly laughs, "Hey, you two should come round to mine Saturday night. You know, because we, unlike Erimentha, actually have friends".

I turn around to give them another stern look and they imitate my narrowed eyes, laughing.

"Do you want to come too?" Beth asks with a grin.

"Of course not," I say, turning round so quickly that the end of my plait hits my cheek, "Why would I want to after the way that you have been treating me today".

"Because you clearly have nothing better to do," Izzy says, "What are your plans for the weekend? Reading dull books about globalisation? Crying that you have no friends?".

"I'll have you know that I am actually seeing a friend on Saturday," I say with my head held high, "We're going to make a working model volcano and I reckon that we will have a substantially more enjoyable, and productive, time than you three".

I hurry off down the corridor, willing myself not to burst into tears. Having read from countless bullying self-help websites, I've been told that these sorts of comments sting like Joseph Lister's carbolic acid against a surgical wound, but I didn't realise that they would be quite so spiteful. I make a note on my sticky pad to ascertain the definition of bullying — it would be nice to give Kimberly and her friends' behaviour a label. I find that things become significantly more manageable when they're given a name. At least then I will have a standard of comparison.

5

"So how was your first day of school?" Mum asks.

"Oh fantastic," I say, "My Geography teacher, Miss Solomon, is amazing. She even wears a pocket protector".

"So *that's* why you've put your Post-Its in your breast pocket," Mum laughs, "What about the girls in your class. Were they nice?".

"Yes, I've made friends with a girl in my form called June," I say, despite the fact that she might not even like me anymore. I didn't manage to catch her in R.S because we had a designated seating plan but I've made a note to talk to her in the morning.

"Cool. That's a nice name as well — you know, June being the best month and all," she jokes, referring to her own Gemini star sign.

"Also, I wonder whether I could invite my new friend Simone round this Saturday afternoon? She loves Geography too and we were going to make a model volcano".

"Sounds good," she says, falling silent for a few seconds as we reach a roundabout.

I am already punching the digits from Simone's scrawled sticky note into her phone when she says, "Can you get her Mum's mobile number so that I can check details?".

"I'm way ahead of you!" I say, trying to decipher the smudged lettering and feeling a slight sense of shame for my Parker pen — it's not used to producing such atrocious handwriting.

I get myself some pumpkin seeds from the pantry when I get home and take them up to my room. Unfortunately for me, and to the delight of my peers, we have not been given any homework apart from writing a brief account of how we found our first day. I take out my 'To Do' notebook, a purple owl pad which Juliet got me for my birthday. I've used it every school evening since April and flick back nostalgically on last year's entries before writing this evening's. I've only been at Lady Nightingale's for a day and yet it feels like seventy full moons have passed since Year Six. I pick up a black Parker pen, title the page and write today's list.

Erimentha Parker's To Do List: Thursday 7th September 2017
- *Do a piece of writing about my first day*
- *Go on a walk in the forest*
- *Research Cambodia*
- *Write a formal plan for my Geography presentation*
- *Ensure that Mum contacts Simone's Mother*
- *Dust bedroom*
- *Print off a method for making a Volcano Model*
- *Sketch out History Timeline for Mr Aldridge*
- *Define 'Bullying'*
- *Read 'The Elegant Universe'*

I prop up the pad on the wall behind my desk and decide to complete my allotted homework first. I hurry downstairs and ask Mum if I can borrow her computer. I usually like to do things by hand but, seeing as it is my first piece, I want to be able to go back and edit it. Not only this, but we've been asked to do no more than two hundred words and if I handwrite it, I just know that I'll go over! Two hundred words just does not seem enough to account for a four hundred and fifty minute long day. Nonetheless, half an hour later, I have condensed my account to fit the exact word limit and, after checking it for grammatical mistakes, I print it off and slide it into a punched pocket so that it doesn't get creased in my satchel. I tick the box on my list with satisfaction and, realising that it will soon get dark, ask Mum if I can now go for a walk in the woods.

"I'm actually cooking dinner at the moment, Erimentha," she says, "But I'm happy for you to go by yourself so long as you stay on the outskirts of the forest. I know I'm worrying over nothing — it's private land after all — but just take my mobile in case there are any problems".

I get changed into something warmer: a pair of cream chinos, a Peter Pan-collared shirt and a green cable-knit jumper which perfectly matches my hair bow from today. Downstairs, I slip on my wellington boots and put a rain hat into my back pocket, alongside my post-it notes and Mum's phone.

"I'm heading off now," I call from the mud room.

"Okay, don't be long. Dinner will be reading in twenty minutes".

I close the door behind me and breathe in the September air, scrunching up my eyes against the long breath of cold as I head across the front garden to the woodland beyond. The wind is blowing from the west and nips at my cheeks, promising to fade the freckles which have formed over the summer. There's something irrefutably refreshing about the chilly air and fallen leaves which crunch with ever greater frequency as I approach the forest. The leaves are mostly green but there is the suggestion of autumn amongst them. I take a few photographs on Mum's phone, capturing the yellows of an oak tree which has been particularly keen on changing its colours. The pistachio of the neighbouring trees seems dull in comparison and only compliments the arrival of the new season. Despite having travailed this forest countless times over the last three years, I still name the trees, saying them aloud as I pass. Holly is easy enough to spot owing to their year-long Christmas festivities, but the first one I pass is male and the waxy epidermal tissue looks lonely without the accompanying red berries. The woodland is mainly composed of oak trees which, whilst rather common in Cornwall, are by far my favourite. I dutifully examine a fallen leaf to determine whether it is a white or red oak — despite already knowing that it is the former. Red oaks are native to North America and don't grow naturally here; the only ones I've seen nearby are at the local Retirement Village where they bought and sowed the seeds themselves. When I last visited grandmama there, I took a sample to examine and made a poster dedicated to the differences between them and those of the white oak. There really is a considerably difference — the leaves of a red oak are a lot larger and sharper and the white oak seems vulnerable in comparison. I snap a quick picture, my frozen fingertips fumbling.

Mum has made pumpkin soup and cornbread: one of my favourite autumnal dishes. The warm cinnamon has settled itself over the kitchen.

"It smells good, Mum," I say.

"Thanks Bumblebee," she returns, "Could you set the table for Nathan and you? I'll call him down in a second".

"Don't worry, I'll run up and tell him. I know you're still getting over that cold".

I walk smartly upstairs and smooth out a crease in the powder blue rug before rapping on my brother's door. He promises his company but I don't hear him getting up from his bed and walk in to hurry him along.

"Mum's spent the last thirty minutes cooking. The least you could do is come down on time for once. After all, it's not like you're doing anything particularly important".

"Actually," he says, "I am building a lego police station. It's taken me nearly the whole afternoon to do and I'm almost finished. I'll only be ten minutes tops".

"Finish it after dinner. You can look forward to it," I say and he reluctantly follows me downstairs.

Mum exaggerates her surprise at having Nathan down on time for dinner, giving him a large round of applause and even pulling back his chair for him as though he's royalty. From what I've read, her being hyperbolic is only counter-productive and will not encourage for him to be on time again. Especially seeing as he's nine, I can imagine that it is just patronising. Although, having said this, I can see a smile peeking at the corners of his mouth. He slurps at the soup but I don't have the heart to tell him off — he's only young, after all, and it's not as though he's ever this rude when we eat out. The sweet steam of pumpkin twists from my spoon, the gamboge orange thick with vegetables and spices. It's hot, but not so hot that it burns my mouth, and the soup is comforting against my tongue, as though you have been wrapped up in a thick duvet. The recipe is my great grandmother's and Mum says that it reminds of her of her childhood Christmases in Paris. For dessert, she makes us each a mug of warm blackcurrant juice which she says that we can drink up in our bedrooms. I take a coaster from my 'homeware drawer' and place it and the mug on my desk, referring back to my To Do list to determine my next task: Research Cambodia. I take a piece of faux parchment paper from my bottom desk drawer and head over to the wardrobe to choose a bottle of ink. I have collected a plethora of colours over the past year and have insofar accumulated six shades:

black, blue, purple, green, red and gold. The pot of black ink is almost empty and so I choose the green instead — it matches school colours, after all — and, using my feather quill, I sketch out the title 'Cambodia' at the top of the paper. I've been trying to learn calligraphy but haven't quite grasped it yet. No matter how many online tutorials I watch, my lettering does not seem to be quite so perfectly formulated as in the videos. It takes me nearly five minutes to write this one word but it looks neat enough and I am happy with it. I take book two of my 1991 Encyclopaedia Britannica set, which fills two whole shelves of my bookcase, and flick through to the page on Cambodia to get a general overview. My nib scratches against the paper — a soprano screech of metal which would, in any other circumstances, be repulsive. I sip at the sweet blackcurrant which warms my stomach as I write. I know that the book's population statistics are outdated, as is the declaration that Pen Sovan is Prime Minister, and I leave gaps so that I can research this on the computer. I use some tracing paper to copy out the map and draw the iconic flag, taking particular care with the intricacies of Angkor Wat. There's nothing about Phsar Chas on the spread and so I instead search for it on Mum's computer. It's rather colourful and I can see why Mr Aldridge said it was the highlight of his trip. Not only are there souvenirs to buy, whose sales boost the local economy, but you can also try national delicacies. From what I can see though, none of it looks particularly appetising, aside from the fruit that is, and I wonder whether he tried anything himself. I photocopy the A4 poster when I'm done to put in my filing cabinet just in case something happens to the original.

I work through the rest of my To Do list with ease and by 1945 hours, I only have my reading and bullying definition left to do. I make a list of the different word meanings that I find:

* * *

Oxford Dictionary: Bully

A person who uses strength or influence to harm or intimidate those who are weaker.

Merriam-Webster Dictionary: Bullying

Abuse and mistreatment of someone vulnerable by someone stronger, more powerful

Cambridge Dictionary: Bully

Someone who hurts or frightens someone who is smaller or less powerful, often forcing them to do something that they do not want to do:

They do not seem to suit my circumstances at all. Yes, in our school environment they may be more popular but this does not necessarily make them more *powerful* than me. Besides, I wouldn't say that I felt intimidated, as the Oxford dictionary says. More than anything, I just feel melancholic at their general dislike for me. I refer to anti-bullying organisations instead — they are, after all, the experts in this field and their definitions are potentially different.

The Anti-Bullying Alliance: Bullying

The repetitive, intentional hurting of one person or group by another person or group, where the relationship involves an imbalance of power. It can happen face to face or online.

Stopbullying.gov: Bullying

Bullying is unwanted, aggressive behaviour among school aged children that involves a real or perceived power imbalance. The behaviour is repeated, or has the potential to be repeated, over time.

There is a definitive emphasis on repetitiveness and, having only been at Lady Nightingale's for a day, it is difficult to ascertain whether this is to be a continuous chain of events. Again, I am forced to disagree on the power imbalance side of things, having been rather secure in my own responses to the girls' comments today; however, Kimberly and Izzy's behaviour is certainly "unwanted" and "intentional". There are echoes of bullying in the events of today but not to the extent that I can confidently assign the label. Instead, I search for 'mean', thinking that this may better meet my needs.

Oxford Dictionary: Mean
  Unkind, spiteful, or unfair.

Cambridge Dictionary: Mean
  Unkind or unpleasant

It is true that today's behaviour was not kind and I certainly did not find it pleasant; however, it wasn't really 'unfair'. After all, it was my know-it-all behaviour which triggered Kimberley's rolled eyes in the first place and if it hadn't been for me sitting with her in Geography, I doubt that the water incident would have occurred. Nonetheless, I decide that I will not let their words faze me. No matter what they do, I will not change. I will continue doing extension projects, even if it means sneaking them to my teachers in the dead of night as though I am a part of some clandestine organisation. I look to the clock and, seeing that it is 2000 hours, I turn off the computer and set it down in Mum's office then run a bath with my absolute favourite body wash. It smells like sweet cinnamon: a paradigm of autumn and I sink low under the spiced bubbles, just as the twilight sky fades to black.

6

I'm up before my alarm again and read in bed until I hear it ring. I'm already one hundred and thirty pages into *The Elegant Universe* and reading all about Entropy. Apparently, the universe is getting more and more chaotic by the day. I wonder if, eventually, there will be no such thing as order at all…

I get dressed quickly and carefully and examine my reflection in the mirror. I've altered the skirt so that it sits exactly on the knee, and I suppose it looks neater this way. My hair pulled back into two neat braids, my baby hairs pushed back with an alice band, and my lips coated with a thick layer of my favourite peppermint chapstick, I pad downstairs for breakfast — quietly so as not to wake my family. I open the kitchen window wide to let in the morning air and carefully make my porridge exactly as I do each morning. I measure, pour and stir, then dollop a heaped teaspoon of sweet blackberry jam on top. I've made it especially milky and its runs from the side of the spoon like cereal, the warm oats spilling into the bowl below. I stir it slowly, listening to the soft pad of morning rainfall, the old oak tree struggling against the wind. Chewing thoughtfully, I sketch out my plan of action for today. I am determined to resolve this silliness between me, Kimberly and Izzy.

Erimentha Parker's Second Day at Lady Nightingale's School for Girls: Plan of Action (non-academic) —

1. Talk with Kimberly, Beth and Izzy — find a time to talk and clarify the exact reason for their unkindness. From here, adjustments can be made as necessary. It is possible that their behaviour is perfectly justified.

2. Talk with Simone about Saturday and details of the project so that tomorrow's construction is as efficient as possible.

3. Talk to June in Form Time about what happened yesterday.

4. Acquire June's email address.

I find June in the classroom when I get to school, writing what what looks like yesterday's homework assignment.

"I completely forgot to do this," she says in explanation. "I thought it would be better to do it now than not hand anything in at all. Mr Aldridge is nice enough but I bet he won't be too happy if he finds out I forgot".

"Yes, you're probably right. Well, at least you're doing it now, I suppose".

She laughs and looks back down to the paper. She probably doesn't want to be interrupted and a knot of guilt secures itself as I continue the conversation.

"Um June. Did Kimberley say anything to you about a water jug by any chance?"

"Yeah, she said that you pushed Izzy", she shrugs, eyes still locked downwards. "But, with her track record, I just assumed that she was lying".

I breathe a peppermint-scented sigh of relief and let my friend get back to her work, offering to check through it when she's finished.

"Seriously, thanks so much Erimentha!" she laughs afterwards. "I still don't know how I managed to spell 'fantastic' wrong. You can tell I was rushing".

"No worries. It happens to the best of us," I giggle as Kimberly and Beth walk in. "Oh and June, I meant to ask — can I have your email address? You know just so that we can talk over the weekend".

Kimberley makes a face at June, "Ew, why would you want to talk to *her*? Haven't we already talked about this, June?"

She laughs as though the two of them are involved in some large joke that I am exempt from.

Instead of reacting, I pass over my sticky note pad and Parker pen to my new friend. It is Kimberley though who picks it up first.

"Why do you carry these around with you, Erimentha? They make you look like a nerd, especially when you put them in your shirt pocket". She sticks out her head and neck and mimes pushing a pair of glasses up her nose. I reach to retrieve the pad but she holds it above her head. Beth laughs.

"You know, you're both being incredibly immature," I say. "I would expect this sort of behaviour from my nine year old brother maybe, but from Year Sevens? I think you're being ridiculous".

Kimberley lowers her arm and head, "Oh Erimentha, I have seen the error of my ways. I hope that you will forgive me".

I know that she's playing the fool, especially seeing as Beth is almost doubling over with laughter, but I simply accept her feigned apology and reach out to retrieve my Post-It notes. As my fingertips graze the slightly waxed paper, she throws it to Beth who, quite to mine and June's disbelief, launches it straight out of the window! It settles on a rooftop below.

"Oh my gosh, Erimentha, I am just so clumsy!" Beth laughs as the bell rings.

"You know, I really think we need to talk through all of this", I say, trying to sound too angry. "Can you two and Izzy meet me here at first break? I think we need to get this sorted".

They assure me they'll be there, declaring hyperbolic apologies for their childish and clumsy behaviour as the rest of the form files in. I take a new pack of Post-It notes from my satchel to replace the martyred stack which now sits atop the tiles of the science block. On the top one I write *Meeting with Kimberley, Izzy and Beth at short break. Form room. Important!*

***

I find it hard to concentrate in history in light of my nerves. In my head, I run over what I will say to them, a butterfly nest forming in the base of my stomach. It's possible that they'll stop being so unnecessarily horrid, and maybe even befriend me, but only if I am able to properly articulate myself. We're learning about the the Battle of Hastings and, as a consequence of my BBC bitesize reading over the holidays, the questions are easy enough and do not require too much concentration. This is lucky because Kimberly, Izzy and Beth's laughter really is quite distracting. Much to my relief, however, they're not talking about me this and are instead running through their plans for this evening's sleepover.

"Okay girls, it's nearly the end of the lesson," Mr Aldridge says, silencing the chatter. "Can you all finish the questions at home and give them to me first thing Monday morning — that's the bad thing about having me as your form tutor: if you don't do the homework, I'll know about it!"

He laughs to let us know that he is not being entirely serious.

"Next lesson we're going to be looking briefly at Oliver Cromwell. Does anybody already know who he is?"

My hand shoots up diligently, straightening so quickly that a shudder passes through my left arm. He calls on Amy instead, me having answered several questions already. She says that he was a ruler in Britain and Mr Aldridge nods carefully. I lift my hand even higher to the ceiling, almost standing up out of my seat. He chuckles at my spectacle but allows me to speak nonetheless.

"Oliver Cromwell was, as Amy quite rightly said, a ruler in England, a position that he acquired as a result of the 1644 Civil War. However, his rule was very oppressive, especially after the extravagancy of Charles I. He established the country as Puritan and banned lots of thing, including music, plays and even Christmas.".

"Perfect Erimentha! You can have a housepoint for that," he says and then, after a final reminder of the homework, he dismisses us for short break and heads off for the staff room.

True to their word, Kimberly, Izzy and Beth remain in the classroom but I don't approach them until the room has been otherwise emptied. I carefully stow away my history book as I wait and ensure that all of my stationery is put away in the correct compartments of my pencil case. The girls' mouths squelch with chewing gum and my stomach twists painfully. I suggest that we sit down, reasoning that imposed formalities will make our whole discussion seem more important. Kimberly sits down on Mr Aldridge's desk chair.

"Well," I say somewhat nervously. "I thought it important to talk with you because I've noticed some tension between us. I feel like you've all been rather unpleasant and that your behaviour is unprovoked. Of course, I may be wrong — you might have a perfectly good reason — and please do correct me if this is the case, but we've only been at school together for one full day and I find it difficult to believe that I could have done something horrid enough to warrant you being so mean. We've already resolved the water incident, but you telling the rest of the form was kind of unnecessary and could quite easily have led to the disintegration of my friendship

47

with June. I am not sure whether you have told the rest of the class yet but—".

"Oh yes, that reminds me. We still need to tell the rest of the form," Beth says. "Thanks for the reminder Erimentha".

"It's that kind of comment which I am finding to be somewhat hurtful," I say calmly.

"What? But we're just joking. Can't you take a simple joke?" Izzy says.

"Yeah, you literally have no sense of humour," Beth chips in. "But I'm not surprised — I mean, you never socialise".

I bite down on my cheek hard to stop myself from crying, but Izzy notices my eyes welling up.

"Beth, that's a bit harsh," she says and my heart lifts momentarily. "I mean, it's not *her* fault that she has no friends".

"But I do have friends," I say meekly. "Take June for example".

"Yeah, I wouldn't bet on her friendship," says Kimberly, who had been strangely quiet until now. "I was talking with her yesterday and she seems to have a *very* different view on your friendship".

"What's that supposed to mean?"

"Don't worry."

"No, tell me."

Kimberly looks down at her nails.

"Besides," she says nonchalantly, "I've already decided that this whole year is going to hate you. If I were you, I'd just accept it".

She gets up to leave but before she opens the door she throws her gum at my shoulder. Strings of still-warm saliva drip complacently from the dun wad of chewing gum, forming a translucent film across the green of my jumper. I don't take it off until the door has closed behind them.

* * *

***

The desks in the English room have been separated in true examination fashion. We're doing a test to determine our ability in the subject and also our sets for the rest of the year. The paper consists of a piece of creative writing and a comprehension task and I find it rather enjoyable. The passage is from *Great Expectations* and I greet Miss Havisham like an old friend. Even *her* company seems comforting after Kimberley's spiteful words at break. I write right up until the last minute, checking my work for grammatical mistakes and ensuring that my story is inclusive of all essential elements, using a sticky note checklist as a guide.

Things to include in my Creative Writing:
- *A beginning, a middle and an end*
- *Conflict*
- *Complex vocabulary*
- *'Real' Characters (ensure that they are more than just two dimensional, impersonal figures)*
- *Use of at least one semicolon*

I jump in my seat when the timer sounds and drop my pen immediately, not wanting to be called on for cheating. I read over my answers as I wait for the papers to be collected and am fairly pleased with my performance; however, am worried that my analysis of the passage was not good enough — I had meant to talk about Estella's callousness towards Pip but simply did not find the time!

My peers grumble about having being given a test on the second day, and even more so when they realise that we have to do the same for mathematics next period. Still in Exam Mode, I manage to complete every calculation, but get muddled on a particularly tricky piece long division and am still worrying about it when June rushes over after the lesson. But I can't stop thinking about what Kimberly said earlier and, guiltily, turn my back, melting into the sea of Year Seven Girls and looking for Simone instead. I catch her in a hug when I see her, reminding myself that, regardless of what they say, I *do* have friends.

"I'm so excited for tomorrow!" she says. "My mom asked if I'm going to be eating dinner at your house. No worries if not, she's just wondering".

"You're welcome to stay for dinner if you'd like — we'd be happy to have you. I was actually thinking that it might be beneficial for us to review that arrangements for tomorrow… you know, so that it's not total anarchy!"

"Even though, anarchy is kind of what we're going for when the volcano erupts," she reminds me with a wink.

"Good point," I laugh. "But I just mean we should go over what materials we need. My Mum says that we can pop out this evening if we need any equipment but there's not point us buying something if you've got it at home".

I pull out my neatly annotated list of Apparatus for the experiment. We have most things at home (apart from brown poster paint, chicken wiring and, seeing as Nathan's allergic, vinegar). Simone agrees to bring the vinegar and even offers her parents' supply of dry ice.

"Then we can make the volcano smoke before it erupts!" she exclaims. "It'll be even more realistic".

7

Simone arrives at exactly 1400 hours and I must say that I am impressed by her alacrity. Her dad drives a Citroen electric car and I go outside to examine it before he leaves. I know a fair bit about the mechanics of the vehicle and am interested to see it with my own two eyes.

"Is your family otherwise Eco-friendly?" I enquire, running my hand along the green car frame. "As in, do you use renewable energy sources to power your home?"

"We've set up a wind turbine in the garden but that only fuels a small percentage of our energy — on a particularly still day, the electricity company will provide us with energy but it's a give and take system. If it is a really windy day and we generate excess, the electricity company will take it. We're hoping to get solar panels installed next month as well".

"Oh, I watched a documentary on solar power last month and have been badgering my parents to get panels installed ever since. Did you know that in seventy years, a rooftop solar panel can prevent the release of *one hundred tonnes* of carbon dioxide? NASA says that CO_2 levels have been on the rise and so it's so important that we reduce levels whenever possible".

I look over to Dad who is shaking his head with a chuckle.

"Maybe we'll see how Simone's family finds the solar panels before making our decision," he suggests.

We leave Mr Randolph and Dad to have coffee and head to the playroom which I carpeted in newspaper this morning.

"This way we can discuss current affairs at the same time," I joke.

All of the supplies are neatly laid out on the side, as well as two lab coats so that we can really feel the part.

"I was thinking that we could film the whole ordeal," I say, picking up the family iPad. "Not only will it make for lasting childhood memories but we could show Miss Solomon".

Simone agrees that this is a marvellous idea and we prop the iPad up on the cabinet to film an introduction I've already scripted. She finds it strange talking to her own image on the screen and keeps on giggling so in the end we scrap this idea and record a voiceover instead. We use Dad's pair of diagonal pliers to cut the chicken wire into fifty-centimetre strips, but, even between the two of us, we're not strong enough to cut it and, with aching palms and lots of giggling, we ask our Dads to help. Sculpting the wire is easier work and we chatter about volcanoes as we form the outline of our mountain. Simone visited Pompeii two Easters ago and her and her family were even able to climb up to Mt Vesuvius's Crater. They even drove up to the Naples Museum of Archeology where she saw the Alexander Mosaic from the House of the Faun in Pompeii, an artefact that I heard about years ago when researching the Romans. It's been on my list of Things to See before I Die since then and I cannot help but marvel at the fact that Simone has seen it in person.

"It was *really* cool," she says. "Even though a few of the pieces were missing."

"I read that there are more than a million and a half different tiles," I say, absent-mindedly straightening the volcano's slope with my palm. "Just think how long that must have taken to craft. He would have had to cut each tessera individually".

"And then you've got us struggling to build a simple volcano sculpture!" Simone laughs, gesturing to the distorted, vaguely-mountainous shape between us.

It's takes longer to perfect the shape than I had anticipated and we mix the PVA glue, water and newspaper in double time to make up for our dilly-dallying.

"Um... Erimentha, you know the paper mache? Do you mind doing it? I want to help but my skin reacts badly to glue," Simone says awkwardly.

"Not at all" I say, picking up a box of disposable gloves. "But I was thinking we could use rubber gloves instead. I didn't really want to get my hands sticky anyway".

We knead the ingredients, discussing our favourite films and laughing as though we have been friends for years. When it's fully coated, I take her outside to show her the garden whilst it dries. It's so cold that you can see our breath and it feels more like December than early September. We sit at the end of the lakeside jetty, examining the motionless water and wavering reeds which cower in the wind like dormice. Simone has borrowed my ski coat and she holds her hands under her armpits to keep them warm.

Earlier, she managed to drip paper mache down the front of her red plaid shirt, despite having worn a button-up lab-coat, and she giggles guiltily when I point it out.

"I've always been quite messy when it comes to arts and crafts," she admits. "In the second grade I managed to spill a whole platter of paints down the front of my dress. My teacher said she'd never met a clumsier girl. I cried so much that they sent me home".

She laughs softly.

"You know, I really miss Arizona. And not just the heat. It's weird when you spend your whole life in one place and then you just move all of a sudden. It's a lot to get used to".

She looks behind her at the house and I watch her. Red hair flies across her face and her left eye twitches slightly.

"And having to go to a new school as well," she turns back to me. "Well, I guess what I'm trying to say is that I appreciate you being so nice to me. You didn't have to say hello to me in the office on Thursday morning, but you did. And I can tell you, that loosened my strings a little. I felt less nervous knowing there were kids like you at Nightingale's. I always went to public school back home and I thought private school would be full of children so privileged that they wouldn't even talk to me".

I feel warm despite the lashings of cold air against my cheeks.

"Mary Wollstonecraft said that nothing is so painful as change," I say. "I think that everyone is finding the transition tricky. I mean, I was kind of nervous about coming to a new school".

Of course, I don't tell her just how nervous I was. My insomnia was so terrible in the first few weeks of the summer holidays that I had to go to my local GP.

"You always seem so... together, Erimentha," she laughs.

A water strider dances across the surface of the lake. I've read that there are around 1700 species of Gerrids and if it weren't so far away I would try to properly identify it. Its legs of thread form a depression in the water, the same groove as when you sit on a particularly supple armchair. Some people call them Jesus bugs because they, like Jesus in Matthew 14:22-23, can walk on water.

"I saw what happened with the water yesterday," Simone says.

I remain silent, examining the barely visible antenna of the insect.

"What happened was annoying, but at least it wasn't

intentional," I say, refusing to make eye contact with my new friend.

"Izzy purposefully poured it on you," she corrects.

I don't say anything. I know that she can't help it but I'm annoyed with her for having seen.

"Erim, I really think that you should tell your form tutor. Not only because of that but because, umm... well I noticed that they were laughing at you at lunch and I could hear them talking about you. I ignored it because you were but I was thinking about it last night and, well, I don't want anything really bad to happen".

I take a measured breath before I respond and will my eyes to brighten into a smile.

"Simone, everything's fine. Izzy says that the water was an accident and I believe her," I say. "I know that you think it's bullying but it's really not".

Yes, they may be being unkind but I'm not lying — after all, I've checked the definition.

"And they were just being silly at lunch," I continue. "You know what girls of our age can be like. Eleven-year-old girls seem to have an innate disposition towards gossiping and I'm sure they didn't mean anything by it. I appreciate that you're just looking out for me but you needn't — everything that you've noted can be logically accounted for".

Simone doesn't look convinced and I see cogs turn underneath the marrow of her skull, beating against the blood flow and electrical impulses of the cerebrum. She is trying to find the right words and any good friend would help her locate them but instead I stand up promptly, my wellington boots slipping slightly on the wood.

"The volcano is probably dry by now. We should go and paint it before your Dad comes".

The volcano truly is something to be proud of and the dry ice makes for a realistic and impressive eruption. Not being entirely sure on how the chemical works, I have written a reminder to research it at a later date. We sketch out a general conclusion together, drawing a few diagrams to show the difference between shield volcanoes and composite cones but the project is nowhere near as bulky as I would have liked and when Simone leaves I spend two hours writing out a six page essay. Using a hole punch and string, I bind the booklet together, tying large bows at the front to secure the paper. It's beautifully aesthetic and I can see why Maria so adored brown paper packages tied up with string. I've also transferred the video we made to a lilac memory stick. I haven't had much practise with editing and it doesn't look awfully professional. Then again, I reason, Miss Solomon will be far more interested in the Geography of the project than any technical specifics and so I try not to worry too much about the shaky cameramanship and terrible audio quality. I did however decide to re-film one of my lines because my lab coat's all bunched up at the front in the original clip. In the new recording, I've kept the coat unbuttoned so that you can see the perfectly-ironed collar of my cornflower blue dress, and redone my high ponytail. Once everything has been checked, named and edited I safely stow the project into an envelope folder, sticking the USB to the plastic with washi tape. I then work on my Hurricane powerpoint presentation until Mum brings up my nighttime mug of warm milk and honey.

"And your teacher asked you to do all this?" Mum asks when I show her.

"Well yes, but she didn't ask *everyone* — it's just that she saw my summer project and asked whether I could show the rest of the class. Of course though, I wouldn't want to stand at the front and ramble without any preparation. I figured that making a presentation would show her just how dedicated I am to her subject".

I am fairly pleased with it and hope that Miss Solomon will be too. In just one lesson she has become my favourite teacher. I'm not even sure what it is that I particularly admire about her — I suppose it's her attitude more than anything. Despite us being new *and* the youngest in the senior school, she made it clear that she was not going to tolerate any silliness when she scolded our table for talking. Perhaps a part of me simply admires that she was able to make Izzy look so scared. As a tribute of sorts to my Geography teacher I've made my own in and out tray, just like hers, out of old cereal boxes. I used acrylic paint to hide the faces of Snap, Crackle and Pop and, despite the slightly jagged edges, have placed it on my desk with pride.

I change into my nightgown when my clock chimes nine. It is embellished with dozens of tiny roses and is long enough that you can comfortably curl your knees up under the fabric. In this exact position I settle into my armchair to read *The Definitive Book of Body Language*, having finished *The Elegant Universe* last night, and I keep The Book of Facts on hand so that I can jot down anything interesting. Perhaps if I follow Allan and Barbara Pease's advice and become more open in my body language, Kimberly and the others will be more friendly with me.

I read a couple dozen pages but cannot stop thinking about what Simone said earlier. What if she tells someone about Kimberly? My parents and teachers would see me as weak (I haven't been able to resolve it myself, after all), and Kimberly would probably despise me even more than she already does.

I set the book down and decide to reorganise my candles. I always keep a few arranged on top of my chests of drawers and bedside table but, aside from the cinnamon scented one, they all breathe floral, summer scents and do not seem appropriate for September's cold temperament. I replace the plum, jasmine and lilac with sandalwood, pumpkin and pine scented wax, using my ruler to make sure that the candles are equally spaced. I am sitting back in my armchair with my journal when Mum comes in to wish me goodnight.

"Nighty night Bumblebee," she says, kissing me on the forehead. "Are you writing about your day with Simone? She's such a lovely girl — reminds me of Juliet".

"They're very different actually. Simone likes art and Geography but Juliet's got no interest in either of those subjects. She just loves history. Do you remember when you and her Mum took us up to the British History Museum and we were telling the curators all about about England under Charles II?".

"I can tell you, they were pretty impressed by that. Most of the other kids were just complaining about how bored they were".

"You mean Nathan," I say smiling, "The only way that you managed to keep him quiet was by promising we'd go to the Lego shop afterwards".

Mum laughs and takes a blanket from my cream ottoman, wrapping it around my shoulders. I rest my chin on my knees, suddenly very tired.

"I'm glad you've already made such lovely friends", she says quietly, kissing me goodnight and leaving me alone with a journal entry nowhere near as lovely as she thinks.

8

On Monday morning, Mr Aldridge tells us our sets for Mathematics and English. The classes are given a colour rather than a number so that we do not know which one is top and which is bottom, but everyone knows that within a few short day we'll have figured out their numerical values. I'm in Mrs Norcop's class for English and I smile in spite of myself. June's friends have commended her as a form tutor and, according to Eleanor Graham, she is one of the kindest teachers in the school. My heart does however sink when I hear Beth's name called out next to mine. I hear the three girls behind me groan.

"You poor thing, Beth," Izzy says. "Having to spend a whole year in the same class as her. Just sit as far away as possible and maybe you won't even notice that she's there".

"Unlikely," Beth says with dismay, "With her hand always in the air, she's pretty difficult to ignore. There's a reason she's called 'Pick-me Parker' after all".

They craft the volume of their voices so that I, but not Mr Aldridge, can hear their stinging words. I turn around quickly.

"I can hear what you're saying and it's really not very—".

"Erimentha," Mr Aldridge says. "Can you save your

conversations for break time. Turn back around please; this is important stuff we're going through".

He's not being entirely serious and I see that his eyes are shining but a bulbous lump still forms in my throat. I can still hear the girls behind, who have miraculously not been noticed by our tutor, but I don't dare tell them off again. I sit up straight in my chair and try to put on a smile but my lower lip trembles and two slow tears trickle down my cheeks. I wait until he's turns to the whiteboard before wiping them away. Kimberly, however, notices.

"Aw, little Erimentha is crying," she whispers with a giggle.

***

I avoid Simone at lunch, still a little upset from Saturday. I am quite sure that Kimberly, Izzy and Beth will indeed be laughing at me in the lunch hall and, if I do sit with her, she's sure to press the issue, insisting that I tell a trusted adult and perhaps even speak to Mr Aldridge. The self-help books all highlight this as the best option but now that I'm in this position myself, it seems as though very little good would come from it. I have insofar formed a confident and near-to-perfect image of myself at Lady Nightingale's and telling a teacher would, as Gordon Kainer said, "liberate like a demolition bomb more than it gives birth to". I smile at having remembered the theologian. Pastor Michael mentioned him in a service a few weeks ago and I dutifully ordered his book *Faith, Hope and Clarity* to my local library. I didn't read the full text but I jotted that line down in The Book of Quotations.

I see June across the lunch hall and she sees me but doesn't come over. On Friday she was friendly and understanding but today she is cold. I saw her talking with Izzy earlier and wonder what they were talking about. Her ringlets bounce as she dashes off to sit with her friends and I turn back to my plate of noodles, chewing absentmindedly on a broccoli stalk as I read *Tess of the D'Urbevilles*.

"Did you know that reading leads to unpopularity?" Izzy says as she brushes past me to put away her tray. "I did a whole research project on it over the summer".

Her voice impersonation is far from realistic but she gets across the message well enough.

"And where, may I ask, did you find this information?" I ask, irritated.

"I read it in the newspaper," she says after a pause.

I am about to ask her which one but she stalks off before I have a chance and it's only when I look back down at my tray that I realise she has taken my flapjack with her.

***

In form-time, the IT technician comes to talk to us through the school email system.

"The email address uses your full name. So, for example, Melody's email will be melodyreed@nightingaleschool.co.uk. Any questions?"

The room remains silent so he continues.

"At the moment, we've set all of your passwords to 'nightingale' and so you'll need to log on this evening and change it to something more secure. If you follow the link on your hand-out, you can change it this evening at home".

I make a note on my Post-It pad so I won't forget.

Mum drives me to tennis straight from school, worried that we're going to be late.

"It starts in four minutes and it's going to take at least another quarter of an hour to get there," she complains. "I think we're going to have to ask for your lesson to be later in future".

The changing rooms are empty and I hurry to get ready quickly. I have chosen a plain white polo and lilac tennis skirt with a matching purple ribbon for my hair. I fold my uniform neatly and Mum takes the bag, giving me a rushed kiss on the cheek before heading off to the cafe. Sometimes she watches me play but it's a little chilly today and so she's getting a coffee instead.

Georgie, my coach, doesn't tell me off even though I'm ten minutes late, and promptly conducts a warm-up game of 'Around the World'. There are only three of us and we have to sprint to keep up with the ball. My cold bones have certainly been warmed after ten minutes. Not having properly practised since July, each of our backhands is a little rusty and we concentrate on fixing this for most of the lesson. My ribbon has started to loosen by the end and I readjust it as we leave to find our parents.

"My new school doesn't finish until 1615," I explain. "And so it's going to be tricky for me to get here on time. If I'm going to continue, I'm going to have to go to a later class".

"No!" Juliet and Lindsay exclaim, insisting that I can't possibly abandon them.

We've all been doing tennis together since Year Three and I know that I would respond in the exact same way if one of them told me they were changing classes.

"Erim, going to different schools is one thing, but leaving tennis means that we'll hardly see each other," Juliet mopes.

"There's nothing I can really do about it," I say regretfully. "But you two could always come to a later class *with* me?"

They promise to ask their parents and I wave them goodbye as I find mine. Mum's just finishing her second coffee and is flicking through a 'Country Living' Magazine. She usually gives them to me when she's done with them.

Some of the pictures, especially in the autumn and winter months, are just so quintessential that I save them for scrapbooking. I keep a stack in my wardrobe.

I ask to borrow Mum's laptop when we get home so I can reset my school email password. It's blustery outside and the internet connection is slow — I have to try three different browsers before I successfully access the webpage. I enter my custom log-in to find six unopened messages. Slightly surprised, I click on the first one which is from Mrs Stafford, my head of year.

I'm very disappointed in you Erimentha. All of your teachers have been saying such positive things about you and it saddens me to discover how inappropriately you behaved today. I would like to see you in my office tomorrow first break and promptly. I will run through your punishment and I advise that you tell your parents this evening because I will be contacting them after our meeting.

You have let both yourself and Lady Nightingale School down.
Mrs Stafford

9

I sit staring at the screen. Its brightness bores into my frontal lobe, inducing a slight headache and I close my eyes to escape the light. It feels as though somebody is pressing their palm against my forehead and I pull my hands up instinctively. In my head, I revisit the events of today, considering all actions which could be considered 'inappropriate'. I certainly did talk during form time, something that is undeniably unacceptable. I scan through the email again, scouting for an indication as to what I have done but the message is far too ambiguous. With a shaky hand, I make a note of my meeting with Mrs Stafford and then turn back to the remaining emails, wondering if they're correlated.

They are.

There are emails from various teachers and a few older students with words such as 'Rudeness' and 'Unbelievable' sitting in the subject box. I wallow in confusion until I find one from a Year Nine girl called Maxine Coppin who lets the cat out of the bag:

You don't have the right to talk to somebody in the way that you did in you're email, let alone an older student. You need to learn how to have some respect Erimentha and so I have forwarded your email to your head of year.

I resist the urge to correct the girls grammar, knowing that it is neither the time nor the place, and instead hover the mouse over the *SENT* box. Twelve emails have been sent on my account and I scroll through them, feeling sick to my stomach. According to this, I have sent a number of hurtful comments to my fellow-students and teachers. I've messaged Maxine telling her she looked like a pig (something I couldn't possibly have reached a judgement on, never having met her!), a long list of emojis to a Year Eleven, and a horrible photograph of a bloody scar to someone in my year. My heart drops when I see that an email has been sent to Miss Solomon. I open it tentatively, preparing to lose her favour.

To Miss Solomon

You're my best friend in the whole wide world (because I don't have any other friends). I want to be just like you and that's why I sucked up to you so much in our lesson. I hope that we will always be best friends.

Love Erimentha xoxo

I should be relieved that the words are not offensive — at least I have not made her feel insecure about herself, as I did with poor Maxine. Nonetheless, I am stained with humiliation. Not only is it informal but the email confesses some sort of undying affection for my teacher. I check that my door is locked before allowing myself to cry.

Mrs Stafford has only *suggested* that I tell my parents and so it is after much thought that I decide not to say anything. Telling them would raise a barrel of difficult questions and would damage my painstakingly crafted persona. It will only upset them and it is surely better for one person to be worried than three?

I end up taking more than my fair share of anxiety, reverting back into July's insomniac state after turning off the light. Dappled moonlight creases my bedspread, peaking through the sides of the curtains and it frustrates me that tonight, of all nights, there had to be a full moon. The opal rays reflect from my filing cabinet, casting a series of swirls across the wall which resemble an ariel photograph of a hurricane. I stare at the ceiling, bending my left arm above my head so I can hold onto the white metal bed frame. It feels cool against my perspiring palms. According to www.anxietycentre.com, you sweat a lot when you are stressed and this is certainly true tonight — I eventually, at three am, I change into a lighter, short-sleeved nightdress.

When I look in the mirror the next morning, the tender epithelial tissue underneath my eyes has been bruised violet and I trace the circles with my fingertips, hoping that they'll not be quite so obvious to everyone else as they are to me. My lips are as parched as August's fields and I apply a generous layer of peppermint chapstick. It stings and I end up wiping it away, coating my lips with vaseline instead. They hang repulsively with slimy petroleum gel and the distinct odour of cocoa butter. I am too tired to tie my french braids and so I leave my hair down, adding a headband to keep it off of my face. Mum has bought me fresh cherries to have with my porridge but, whilst I know for the fruit to be scrumptious, all I can taste is the flavourless whiteness of the milk.

It's Nathan's first day today and the two of them walk with me to the bus stop, bid me farewell and then continue on to St. Agnes's Primary School. As I stand under September's cold blanket, I feel a sudden pang of nostalgia, wishing that I too could be sitting down to Reading Time with Mrs Luton and Juliet this morning instead of venturing back to a school which has quickly become terrifying.

I head to the staff room as soon as I get in, still holding my satchel and PE bag. A teacher with curly red hair answers the door and asks me brightly who I am looking for. On any other day, I would respond with an equally wide smile but I cannot bring myself to it.

"I'm wondering whether Mr Aldridge is in there please," I say politely. "I'm Erimentha Parker. I'm in his form".

When I say my name, her smile fades slightly but she agrees to get him nonetheless. My form tutor looks taller than ever and I wonder if he too was tossing and turning under the brightness of the full moon. He is wearing a cream suit, similar to Jay Gatsby's.

"Um... Mr Aldridge, I really need to talk to you about something. I hope you're not busy".

He nods softly and leads me to an empty psychology classroom a few doors down. There is a large diagram of the brain taped to the back wall and I resist the urge to examine it in more detail.

"Erimentha, I don't know what to say to you," he says, running his hands through his hair. "I received an email from Mrs Stafford and, more than anything, I think I'm just surprised".

I turn to the window and crisp autumn sunlight seeps through the glass and warms my skin.

"You're a bright girl, Erimentha", he continues sternly. "Why *on earth* did you think sending those emails would be a good idea?"

I bite down hard on my cheek hoping that it will stave off any tears.

"That's exactly what I wanted to talk to you about, Mr Aldridge," I say shakily. "You see, yesterday, when I logged onto my email account to change the password, I found these emails on my account and, well, I never sent them!"

I bite down again on my cheek but it doesn't stop the tears.

"I would never do anything so spiteful. It made me feel ill just looking at how horrid the messages were".

I apologise and pinch the back of my hand in an effort to

silence my tears. He waits for my sobbing to subside and wrings his hands uncomfortably.

"So you really didn't send those emails, Erimentha?" he asks.

I shake my head furiously and he takes a long, deep breath. His nose hairs quiver in the artificial breeze.

"In which case, we're going to go and find Mrs Stafford right now because if you are telling the truth, this is very serious".

He pops into the staffroom on the way over, asking somebody to register the form, and we then hurry over to Mrs Stafford's office. His strides are long and I am almost running to keep up.

"Erimentha, I must point out that if you are lying to me about this I will not take it lightly and I can assure you that the consequences will be severe. Maybe even suspension".

Mrs Stafford is on the telephone and Mr Aldridge waves through the door to let her know that we are here. I hear her apologise through the receiver, evidently finishing her conversation earlier than intended. She ushers us in quickly.

"I thought I told her to come at short break?" she says to Mr Aldridge breathlessly.

"Yes, you did, but Erimentha came and found me first thing and she says she didn't send those emails".

Mrs Stafford turns to me, her face stern and her lips pursed, and I take this as my cue.

"I logged on yesterday evening to change my password and found a number of unopened messages. I was shocked to see your email, and even more shocked when I looked at the emails which had been sent on my account. I promise you that I wasn't the one who sent them".

I say this all rather quickly and my words roll over themselves. I have never been in proper trouble before.

"I'm not saying I don't believe you, Erimentha, but before

we look into this, I need to be sure that you are telling the truth. Is there any way you can prove what you are telling us?"

I fall silent for a second, a crease appearing on my forehead as I contemplate the question.

"Yes!" I exclaim, much more loudly than intended. "You see, I had tennis yesterday evening and didn't get home until 6pm. I logged onto my emails as soon as I got home but, by this time, the messages had already been sent. Thence, they must have been sent before I got home! My Mum would tell if you were to ask".

I falter at this point, however, and Mr Aldridge asks what's wrong.

"It's just, well, I didn't really want my parents to know. You see, they would only worry unnecessarily. Is there any way that you could talk to her without actually saying what happened with the email server?"

The two teachers look at one another, looking uncomfortable.

"We really should tell your Mum and Dad, Erimentha," Mr Aldridge says. "What has happened is terrible and very hurtful. I think that need to know".

"However," Mrs Stafford continues, "if it's really that important to you, we can let this one slide. But if anything else happens, I will have no choice but to tell them".

"I don't think that they meant anything particularly malicious by it," I say, looking down at my feet. "I expect that they thought it all to be rather funny. Do you think we'll even find out who did it?"

"It's difficult to say because the emails were sent after school hours," Mrs Stafford says reluctantly. "But we will try our best to find out. Can you think of anybody who holds a particular grudge against you?"

I think of Kimberly, Izzy and Beth but shake my head.

"Alright, Erimentha," Mr Aldridge says. "Do you want to head to your next lesson? We've only got a few minutes until the bell rings now. And I promise to sign you in".

He says this last bit with a smile and I grin back at him, hauling myself and my two bags out of the office.

I walk leisurely to Religious Studies, feeling considerably lighter after the meeting but still rather shaky as I contemplate just how much trouble I could have been in. There is a Year Eleven form in the classroom and I wait outside for them to file out, reading from a display about Descartes's perception of the self. I've heard the famous *Cogito Ergo Sum* in passing, of course, but this is the first time that I've seen the name of a corresponding philosopher and I make a note of him on a Post-It note for later research. Most of my form arrives before the bell rings, having left early in Mr Aldridge's absence.

"Where were you?" Melody asks curiously.

"Oh, I was asked to talk with a few teachers is all".

The bell rings and the Year Eleven form files out, pushing each other with far more laughter, shouting and pushing than I would've expected from fifteen year olds.

"Was it about the emails that you sent, Erimentha?" Kimberly says loudly and it feels as though everybody in the vicinity looks her way. I shudder involuntarily but meet her eye with, what I hope to be, confidence.

"Everyone's talking about it," she explains.

Most of the older girls look disinterested and stalk through the crowd of parted Year Sevens, nostalgically discussing their own arguments in lower school.

"Do you remember how we were that age?" One of them giggles. "I still can't believe that you spilled that whole pot of fuisha paint on my shirt. My mum was so mad at me!".

A brief shudder of hope rushes up my vertebral column. Perhaps one day Kimberly and I will remember these first days as nothing more than playful banter. Looking at those pale blue irises, it somehow seems unlikely.

"So you're the kid who send Kalyn all those smiley faces!" One of the remaining Year Eleven girls laughs.

"Agh that was so annoying!" the girl who I assume to be Kalyn says. "I can't believe you had the nerve to send it".

I see Kimberley smirking from behind her back.

"But no hard feelings — I was the same when I was in Year Seven," she smiles before walking off with her friend.

Eleanor Graham told me to steer clear of the Year Eleven girls but, from what I've just encountered, they seem to be more good-natured than those in my own year group! Kimberly looks disappointed — clearly she was expecting a confrontation. She turns her back on me, talking with Izzy loudly about my 'too-long skirt', but I just raise my head high and walk into the classroom.

***

I find Miss Solomon at lunch. Thankfully, she's in her classroom, chewing absent-mindedly on a sandwich that I assume to be tuna owing to the salty smell which hangs over the classroom like steam over hot chocolate.

"Just give me a second, Erimentha," she says, typing furiously on her computer. Her nails are unnaturally short and she clicks ENTER with such force that the key would echo if were we in a larger room. She swivels her desk chair to face me.

"Miss Solomon, I know you received an email from me last night," I say, carefully watching her reaction, "and I just wanted to explain myself".

"No need, Erimentha. Mr Aldridge has already told the staff what happened. It's horrible that anybody would do this. Do you have any idea who it could be?".

She asks this next question more gently, probably hoping to pass something onto Mrs Stafford, but I simply shake my head. Whilst I'm ninety percent sure it was Kimberly, it's a serious accusation. Yes, she has been beastly this last week but nobody deserves to be blamed for something they didn't do.

10

Nervous that she'll ask me about Kimberly again, I don't speak to Simone all week — aside from the occasional rushed hello in the corridor. She starts spending more time with Melody and, by Thursday, she does nothing more than smile when we pass by each other. With June ignoring me, I spend each lunch break in the library (which isn't really anything to complain about!). Rarely busy and always quiet, it only takes me a few days to realise that I am not the only one using this room as a sanctuary. The little girl with the dark fringe sits with a Pink Spinner book every afternoon, curled up in the same purple armchair. Ms Athena says that she is in Year Five and it surprises me that she is older than Nathan — after all, he must be almost four inches taller than she is. Even accounting for the fact that girls are shorter than boys until around eleven, the height difference is staggering. There is something rather solemn in the little girl's demeanour, and I wonder if something is worrying her. Then again, it might be nothing in real life at all. I don't know what she's reading about and it is difficult not to look sad if you're protagonist has just lost a parent.

***

* * *

Miss Solomon reminds me about my Geography presentation on Thursday, not that I had forgotten. I transfer the presentation to her computer and take a deep breath, lifting my shoulders up towards my ears with a dimple-embellished smile.

"Hurricanes," I begin, "are given different names according to where in the world they occur. For example, in Asia, the correct term is a cyclone. You may also be surprised to know that gales are our own equivalent and windspeed is occasionally great enough that, were we in the US, it would be classified as a hurricane".

I work through the powerpoint with a clear and confident voice and, when I have finished, I am gifted a round of applause led by Miss Solomon. Kimberly and Izzy give me a standing ovation, whooping with evident falsity. My teacher frowns at them and, as with last week, I am impressed by how quickly the two subside. When I sit back down at my desk Kimberly leans over and taps me on the forearm. Her fingers are cold and so her circulation is probably not very good. Maybe she doesn't get enough exercise.

"Erimentha, do you ever go looking for hurricanes?" she asks. "You know, to take pictures and stuff".

"I never have actually. The life of a storm chaser can be a dangerous one. Did you hear about Tim Samaras who went after one in Oklahoma and was killed".

"Oh that's a shame," she grimaces. "So no chance of the same thing happening to you then?"

I try to concentrate on my worksheet but her comment is not eroding quite so quickly as the Holderness Coastline. They throw little pieces of scrunched up paper my way, scattering my desk surface with snowflakes, each one torn off hastily and irregular. I see little raindrops of saliva, indebted with pathogens, land amongst them as they giggle. What

most annoys me is that there is no originality to the deed —
the boys at primary school would spend class time messing
around in the exact same way and, in a way, I pity their
immaturity. They pelt a larger ball of paper towards my head
and it bounces from my forehead onto the desk. Irritated, I
unfurl it to retrieve their message: *I can't believe you're ignoring
us. You're so mean. No wonder you have no friends.* I make brief
eye-contact with Izzy before asking Miss Solomon if I can go
and get a drink of water.

"I'm not feeling my best," I explain and it's not really a lie.

In the bathroom, I fix the hair clips in my ponytail and
tighten the hairband. I try smiling at my reflection but there is
something dull in the face that greets me. Cheerfulness does
not crease her eyes and she looks sad. Anybody even
remotely observant would know that her smile wasn't
genuine. I wash my hands well and turn off the tap with my
sleeve, having read about just how many germs can be found
on the handle. True to my word, I take a long drink from the
water fountain, feeling the cool water against and down the
back of my throat. My stomach feels full after a few seconds
and I wonder just how much water it takes to kill a person. I
make myself a note on my Post-It pad to find out. Miss
Solomon meets me as I'm walking back up to the classroom.

"I was just coming to check you were alright, Erimentha,"
she explains.

"Oh thank you. Yes, I'm all okay now".

"Well I'm glad to hear it but if you feel any worse, just let
me know and I can send you to the nurse. You do look a little
peaky now that I think about it. I'll tell you what, I'll go and
get you an orange from the staff room and you can snack on
that during the lesson".

"Alright girls, I just need to go and get something from
downstairs," Miss Solomon says. "I'm trusting you all to be
quiet this time".

She looks at us sternly before leaving the classroom and I stay by her side until she departs, not wanting to disturb the silence. My table's giggles echo as the door closes and my breath catches as I see the carnage of my desk. My Parker pen has leaked over my worksheet, smothering the neat annotations in a puddle of ink which is already starting to dry. My pencil case, which was previously propped up neatly on my textbook, lies in the middle of the page and the cream fabric has been stained blue at the bottom. I use my fingertips to peel back the zip and carefully extract my stationery, hoping that it has not completely bled through. My rubber is stained beyond recognition, as are two of my pencils, but everything else can be salvaged. Using only the tips of my fingers, I unscrew the pen and the ink cartridge drops out immediately. It has been partly cut in half and is practically empty, dripping with ink which stains my fingertips. This giant mess of ink was clearly not an accident. I meet the gaze of Kimberly who has been watching me with a strong sense of satisfaction but I break quickly from her cold, pale eyes and use a tissue to mop up the ink before it irreversibly damages the desk. The pool of blue seeps lazily into the thin paper and it reaches my fingertips, staining them indigo. I manage to mop up most of the ink and put the sodden bundle of blue into a zip-lock bag, but the desk is still blue when Miss Solomon returns. I am still scrubbing desperately, merely smearing the colour across the surface, when she places the orange on my desk. The classroom is once again completely silent.

"What happened?" she stutters, looking utterly shocked.

"Erimentha was trying to show us this trick with her pen but it landed on the desk and just exploded," Izzy exclaims with wide, innocent eyes.

"We tried to tell her it wasn't a good idea but she wouldn't listen to us," June says, avoiding my eye.

"Is this true, Erimentha?" Miss Solomon asks sternly.

I go to say something but feel my voice breaking. It catches in the back of my throat and and pulls against my epiglottis. I look towards the floor, not wanting them to see how flustered I am.

"She's only crying because she doesn't want to get into trouble," Kimberly says matter-of-factly.

Miss Solomon tucks her hair behind her right ear and asks me to step outside with her.

"I leave the room for two seconds, Erimentha. Can you tell me honestly what happened with that pen? I find it hard to believe that you were throwing it around. I heard you telling off Daisy earlier for throwing around hers!"

"I wasn't throwing it around," I whisper. "In fact, I don't know what happened".

"I suppose it was just an accident then. In which case, I'm not mad at you, Erimentha. We all make mistakes".

I nod, the lump loosening in my throat, "I promise to clean it all up".

"I don't doubt that you will".

She looks at me very carefully and opens her mouth very slightly but quickly shakes her head, thinking better of what she was going to say. I sit back down at my desk and can feel Miss Solomon watching me as I scrub at it with my baby wipes, not even touching the orange.

11

After school on Friday, we go food shopping where Mum says I can choose a special Friday snack.

"It's been a long week!" she says with an exaggerated huff and it takes me a few seconds to realise that she is not referring to my week, but her own. Evidently, Mrs Stafford stayed true to her word because my parents never mentioned anything about the email scandal. I make a note on my sticky note to write a thank you letter of some kind to her and Mr Aldridge.

I choose a blueberry Nature bar and a carton of banana milk. Mum gets Nathan a chocolate milkshake and some chocolate buttons.

"Gosh, he is going to be hyper tonight!" she says.

"Sugar doesn't actually trigger hyperactivity in children — it's just an Old Wives' Tale of sorts," I correct. "The people who make sugar-laced children's snacks must be really annoyed that everyone thinks it does!"

We venture down the frozen goods aisle and I pull my blazer more tightly across my chest to keep warm.

"I always forget how chilly it can get in here," she laughs, browsing the selection of ravioli. "Do you want me to get some mushroom pasta, Bumblebee?"

Before I have a chance to answer, a middle-aged lady closes in from behind and steals Mum's attention.

"Oh Julia, it's been forever!" the woman exclaims. "Did you have a good summer? We were in Bali for the whole first month and Ella, bless her, almost burnt to a crisp".

She motions to the child standing behind her. It's the little girl from the library. She gives me a shaky smile but quickly returns her gaze to the floor.

"Listen, we're having a barbecue on Sunday," the lady continues. "Just a few families as a New School Year celebration of sorts. You, Mark and the kids are welcome to come if you're free".

"That sounds wonderful," Mum says. "What time?"

"Around eleven? But it's an all day thing so just pop in whenever".

I flinch at the informality of the invitation.

"Let's just hope the weather holds up, eh? This rain is such a pain after all that sun".

"You say that," Mum laughs, "But Erimentha is always happiest when it's cloudy. This is her favourite weather".

The lady glances at the dull grey clouds behind her, not looking convinced.

"Are you going to be continuing with aerobics this term?" she asks. "I've had to pull out unfortunately. My physician says it's not doing my back any favours".

She throws her head back in a laugh.

"I'm actually stopping too." Mum says. "I've heard that Yoga is the way to go and so Erimentha and I took it up this summer".

"I love it," I add. "Since taking it up I've noticed a vast improvement in my posture".

I catch Ella staring at me and I smile at her again. The lady looks at me too.

"You've just started at Lady Nightingale's, haven't you? In

Year Seven? How are you enjoying it?"

"Yes, it's great," I say, "I'm especially impressed by the teachers — they're all lovely".

"Don't forget the girls," she laughs, ruffling Ella's hair so that her fringe sticks up. "I've got two there at the moment — one of them is in your year actually. Kimberly".

"Kimberly Barton?"

"That's the one!" the lady laughs.

She starts to say something about it being a small world but I am no longer fully listening. Mum has just agreed to attend a barbecue at *Kimberley's* house. I try to restore a sense of calm, reasoning that a barbecue could be the perfect place to form a friendship and put an end to all of this silliness at school. I force a smile and am disappointed by the uncanny optimism in my voice.

"Oh yes, Kimberley's in my form actually," I say. "We sit together in Geography".

"Good friends already. That's what I like to hear. Quite the social butterfly isn't she?" she says to Ella who nods half-heartedly. "I'm sure Kimberly'll be over the moon to see you on Sunday".

She shoots us a hurried goodbye, explaining that they don't have long left on their parking ticket and I wave to Ella.

"She's a bit over-the-top," Mum says, "But they're a lovely family really. I'm so glad that you and Kimberley have hit it off".

12

I visit my grandmother at Oakwood Retirement Village on Saturday afternoon. My family rarely accompanies me on these visits. It's not that they don't *enjoy* seeing Grandmama — of course they do — but it's difficult for them to find time in the hustle and bustle of twenty-first century life. Knowing that she doesn't get many outside visitors, I try to see her at least once a fortnight. Like me, Grandmama is an avid bookworm and has two large shelves crammed so full of books that the back of the cupboard can hardly be seen. The titles vary from stories to autobiographies to poems to atlases — and they're not only in English. She is fluent in no fewer than five languages, and partially fluent in a further seven. She's forever encouraging me to pick up a new tongue myself but I have never found the time. I speak French, of course, but that's only because Mum grew up in Paris.

The walk across the carpark leaves me nearly frozen and I find myself hoping that the Bartons' barbecue will be cancelled. I shake my head. Wishful fulfilment will not do.

"Hi Erimentha, how are you?" the receptionist asks when I enter the lobby.

"Oh hello, Celia," I reply. "I'm very well thank you. I wonder whether I could see Elizabeth Leroy? Is she available?".

"Of course she is, darling. I expect that she's waiting for you".

I walk out onto the cobbled pathway where bicycles sometimes roam. The individual apartments are like the ones that I built with wooden blocks as a young child: simple and symmetrical. There are large black lanterns outside each room and, despite it being four in the afternoon, the early-risen twilight means that they have been switched on. Warm yellow lights pierce the heavy September mist and cast a dim glow through the haze. The tennis courts peek out from behind a tall alder tree and it really does look rather picturesque. I hope that my children will send me some place similar when I retire. I expect my cheeks are as red as cherry tomatoes in the bitter wind and I feel them with the back of my hand — my cool fingers burn against the sensitive tissue. Grandmama's room is not too far a walk from the reception and has an excellent view of one of the dining rooms, a rectangular building with the same yellow lights expelling from every surface. It resembles some sort of Victorian circus with its pointed roof. On the porch outside of her room, there is a small letter box, similar to the kind that American families have in television shows, and I slot the letter that I wrote earlier down the side. I write her a short message every time I visit and she sends me her reply in the post. I would like to have the postman deliver my letters too but the stamp-cost is simply too high (no way could it be covered by an eleven-year-old's pocket money!). Grandmama has assured me that she prefers it this way — she says it's charming.

"Oh Erimentha, how wonderful that you are here," She exclaims when she opens the door. "And don't you look lovely today — even more so than usual, I might add!"

I look down peevishly at my long-sleeved yellow top and patterned skirt. I've had the latter since I was about eight and it is covered with dozens of tiny soldiers, each one standing to attention in a little red coat.

"Thank you and, to return the compliment, I must admit that I do love that shade of green on you!" I say, referring to her floral chiffon blouse.

She laughs deeply and then sits down on the side of her bed. We made the quilt together a few years ago and the side closest to the window has been singed white by the sun.

"I know it's rather cold out but I was thinking that we could go on a stroll around the grounds today?" I suggest. "As Mum would say, it's been rather a long week and it would be pleasant to take a look at the Red Maple. I brought the camera so that we could take photographs as well".

She agrees that this is a lovely idea but, then again, she always does. I think she just appreciates my company and so, as long as I'm not insisting upon taking a trip outside of the complex, she remains content. It's not that she wants to completely isolate herself from the outside world but her dissolving eyesight means that she can no longer drive and she never really was a fan of buses. She always gets scared they'll break down. When she comes round for Christmas dinner and the like, she always insists we pick her up directly.

Grandmama bundles herself up in a warm ski coat, the same one she wears on our annual trip to the Alps. She mainly sticks to the gentle blue slopes nowadays but, as a young woman, my Mum told me that she would attempt even the most dangerous and icy slopes. I've got to say, I'm glad she's no longer so reckless — after all, an average of forty two people die each year in such accidents.

Grandmama wears her apartment key on a lanyard around her neck and I've always been impressed by its practicality. Having noticed how much I liked it, she bought me my own one last January; however, I don't use it anywhere near as much as I thought I would. I tried attaching a pad of sticky notes to the metal crocodile clip but, unsurprisingly, it didn't work very well.

Outside, the wind bites at our cheeks, nipping at my nose like an excitable puppy, and I clench my fist to my chest to protect myself from the chilly breeze.

"This cold afternoon will turn us all into fools and madmen," Grandmama murmurs, pulling her wooly hat further over her ears.

"Is that Shakespeare?"

Grandmama's wide breadth of reading means that you can never be quite sure where she is quoting from. One minute she will be whispering the words to Dickinson's 359 and the next she'll be chanting an amusing piece from a Bill Bryson novel.

"Any more specific?"

I look down at my mustard yellow Maryjanes, rattling through the few Shakespeare plays that I have read. I certainly recognise the line and expect I jotted it down in The Book of Quotations whilst reading.

"King Lear?" I try.

She nods encouragingly, now asking me for the exact Act and Scene. The second answer having been a guess, I admit defeat and deflate like an untied balloon released from a child's sticky fingertips.

"Even getting the play right is impressive, Erimentha," she assures me. "Very few girls your age have read it, I am sure. Oh, that reminds me actually, I was looking through my bookshelf on Tuesday and I found my copy of *Much Ado About Nothing*. I think you'd love it — Beatrice is just as headstrong as you (though not as polite, I might add!)".

I delightedly thank her for the suggestion and write a reminder on my sticky pad to collect the play before I leave. Grandmama points towards the river and nostalgically recalls the summer before last when Nathan, the other grandchildren and I had bathed in the cool water. It had been dreadfully hot that July and the river level had so far diminished that the adults had deemed it safe to swim in. I had never gone wild swimming before and, whilst I knew for the far-off crickets and laughing children to be idyllic, a part of me was still rather nervous of the rocks on the river bed. I had picked myself carefully across the mud, using my big toe to tentatively check for sharp pebbles before putting my foot down completely. An old man ended up lending me his tape measure so that I could measure the height and width of the river at different points. Grandmama later showed me how to calculate the hydraulic radius. I composed a small project for her on my findings and bound it with ribbon. My handwriting was far from neat but she still has it propped up on her dressing table. It seems that I couldn't even use a ruler properly for the diagrams are all muddled. The colouring is excellent though, if I do say so myself. I was always one to meticulously stay within the lines and was even given a special certificate for it when I was in Reception. It was the first one I was ever given and Dad framed it and hung it up on the wall.

There are picnic tables on the grass, sodden with damp and already starting to grow lichen as some sort of shield against the fast-approaching winter. The green flecks sit like miniature stalagmites on top of the oak, nestling in the slits between the wooden boards. There are holes for umbrellas in the middle, but these are invariably not being used today. I wonder whether they will be used at all again before April. The tree branches stutter in the breeze and a few of the leaves are torn from their stalks. They dance through the air lazily, twirling and swooping like swallows, before landing gently on the grass: a stark brown contrast against the green. They look so very carefree — probably because they do not have an obligation to attend a barbecue with a girl who quite clearly hates them.

"If you run over to the pool and ask for a basket, we can collect acorns, pinecones and the like," Grandmama suggests and I dutifully dash off, my duffle coat flapping and my high ponytail swinging behind me.

"Excuse me," I say breathlessly to the gentleman manning the poolside. "You wouldn't possibly have a basket, would you? My Grandmother and I are hoping to collect some things from the woodland".

"Of course," he says, passing me a waterproof basket from behind the desk. "You know, it's so lovely that you're here seeing your Grandma. A lot of the Old Folks don't get any visitors and you can't help but feel sorry for them. At least they've got each other though. So many residents that it makes sense they all become friends".

"Yes, I suppose so," I say softly, taking the basket.

I bid him farewell and ponder over his last comment as I leave the vicinity, wishing that I could make friends just like the elderly residents here. Through the glass, I glimpse three ladies chattering in the shallow end of the pool, each wearing a block colour swimming costume, and I cannot help but envy their carefree smiles. I have Grandmama of course, and Juliet, but I am pretty sure that I have permanently lost June and Simone, and it would be lovely to have just one friend to talk and sit with at lunch. Grandmama is holding her hands under her armpits when I return.

"Curses, I should have brought gloves!" she laughs.

She then looks at me very carefully for a few seconds.

"Why, Erimentha, what is the matter? What has happened to your smile and skipping steps? Was it that Jenny lady on duty at the pool? Gosh, she can be horrid sometimes — very patronising, if you ask me. One time she insisted that I used a pool float! Me! Can you imagine?"

So there were mean girls even at Grandmother's age.

"Grandmama, I wonder whether you have any friends here?" I ask.

Perhaps she is like me and doesn't have any special friend at all. Perhaps she is picked on by Jenny in the same way that Kimberly picks on me. I know that not all adults are pleasant — you only had to read one Dickens novel to find that out — but it never occurred to me that petty unkindness could occur even at seventy-odd years.

"Hmm... Well, I don't know whether I'd call them friends".

I feel my heart lift and feel terrible for it.

"But I do have a few close acquaintances. My only true friends are stacks of books and a loving family".

She puts her hand on my shoulder and I can barely feel her fingertips through my thick hood.

"What about meanness? You said that there was Jenny, but... is there anyone else who is unkind?"

"Now listen to me, Erimentha. There will be unkindness wherever you go but that does not mean there are unkind people".

I nod slowly.

"So unkindness is only temporary?"

"Yes, I believe it is," she says and I look up at the Red Maple whose leaves have only just started to tinge. "I'm not going to tell you that I have lived a morally perfect life because I haven't. When I was a little girl, I would pinch my sister when my mother wasn't looking. But does this make me an unkind *person*?"

I shake my head, "No. Because you are kind at other times".

"And that's exactly it. Sometimes we're kind and sometimes we're not. Some people just lose sight of the good inside of them".

"Can we help them find it again?"

"Well, yes. At least that's what Bonhoeffer said we should do," she says, looking dreamily over at the picnic tables, deep in thoughts that I wish I too could see. "But it's not always easy, Erimentha. An no-one can expect you to do it. It can seem near to impossible to completely reform somebody".

Grandmama is quite right — people probably aren't *expecting* me to, but if I can change Kimberly for the better, my happiness too will be improved as a natural consequence. Of course my motives are slightly less altruistic than Bonhoeffer perhaps intended but the end result at least will be more than positive. I pick up a pinecone which has rolled to my feet and place it gently in the basket.

13

"What fire is in mine ears? Can this be true?".

I'm standing in the middle of my bedroom in a pair of button-up flannel pyjamas, acting out *Much Ado About Nothing* with Grandmama's script held in my hand. I pelt out Beatrice's lines with bravado, already having warmed to the witty heroine. Mum walks in to wish me goodnight and watches my little one-woman show for a few minutes, clapping when I reach the end of the next scene. I respond with a low stooping bow, pretending that I am in the Globe Theatre.

"You're just like my mum," she laughs. "She'd read Shakespeare after putting Edith and me to bed and her echoing performance would keep us up for hours. I never understood the appeal of Shakespeare if I'm completely honest... but don't tell Grandma!"

"Grandmama," I correct. "And don't worry I won't".

She gives another little laugh and reties her dressing gown cord.

"We'll be coming back home after church before heading over to the Barton's house for the barbecue. I've asked, and Grace says not to get spruced up: it's all very casual".

I nod absent-mindedly, my anxiety spreading like party

streamers. I briefly consider feigning illness but, as far as I see it, lying is morally wrong and always brings about more harm than good.

"Why don't you choose your outfit now so that you're not in a rush tomorrow?"

Despite being sleepy, I agree. *Psychology Today* says that clothing plays a vital role in first impressions and, despite having already made mine, this is still the first time that she will see me wearing *home* clothes. I bid Mum goodnight and then head over to the wardrobe. I leaf through hangers of pleated skirts, deciding eventually on a pretty green one, and pair it with a white Peter Pan-collar shirt and olive-green button-down cardigan. I also hang up my clothes for church, (a white linen dress, lilac cardigan and matching oversized bow. I hope that Mum will wear her purple dress so that we will be matching). I straighten the clothes hangers, clean my face with help from the wash basin, and fall to sleep almost immediately.

***

I decide to teach myself Morse Code before breakfast. I print off the alphabet and practise tapping out words, lying on my rug still in my pyjamas. On Sundays we wait until after breakfast before putting our church clothes on — it's something that my Dad would do when he was young and I suppose that it has become a *shibboleth* of sorts (I learnt that word yesterday from Grandmama and it's now one of my favourites!). My room is looking especially clean this morning, but the small wrinkles in my duvet cover are illuminated by the blinding white sky. I borrow the travel iron from the utility room to smooth down the sheets and they are soon as flat as skimming stones.

I am fairly good at Morse Code by the time that I am called

down for breakfast but still need to occasionally refer to my print-out. I demonstrate this new skill over the dining table and Dad taps out a reply, having learnt it for after lights out when he was at boarding school.

"Alright troops," Mum says. "We've got just under an hour until we leave. Can we make sure that we've got everything ready for later because we're only going to have a five minute turnaround between church and the barbecue".

I help Dad with the dishes, wearing a pair of extra small blue rubber gloves.

"Are you sure you would like to go today?" I ask him hesitantly. "I mean, it's not really prime weather for a barbecue".

"It's actually not as cold as yesterday and, whilst it's cloudy, no rain is forecasted. I thought you'd already have checked BBC weather, Erimentha?"

"Oh I have. But barbecues are usually done in the heat and, well, perhaps it will not be too enjoyable in the cold".

"Listen darling," he says. "If I'm completely honest, I'm not too keen on this meal either but Grace is a good friend of your Mum's and we have to make an effort for her sake. I know she'd be really upset if we missed today".

I feel terrible all of a sudden. Mum does so much for me and I can see that I realise that I'm being really rather selfish. My friendship problems with Kimberly shouldn't stop her from having a jolly good time today. I thank Dad for his words and get ready for church, trying to ignore the biting mass of nerves which has formed in my stomach. I am going to have a pleasant time today, I assure myself. By the end of the afternoon, Kimberly and I will be thick as thieves.

14

"You have heard it said, 'eye for an eye, tooth for a tooth' but I tell you this, turn the other cheek". Jesus wants for us to be forgiving of our enemies, acceptant of their apologies and able to move on. Let us not be bitter and revengeful but able to accept our fellow man".

Pastor Michael's words ring with the doorbell when we arrive to Kimberly's house. I must forget the events of the last two days and approach today with a clear head.

"Oh Julia, I'm so happy that you came!" Grace air-kisses my mother with forced gaiety.

I notice that despite her insistence on casual wear she is wearing a sequinned brown dress. I internally criticise the silk, knowing that silkworms were boiled alive to obtain the fabric.

"The other kids are in the front room," she says to Nathan and me. "We'll be going outside in a bit. We're hoping that the weather will pick up in the next hour".

She leads us to their lounge which is extravagantly furnished with deep brown leather sofas and a large television set. There are six other children littered on the floor.

"Oh hi Erimentha!" Kimberly says with such enthusiasm

that I blink. "It's *so* amazing that you were able to come today".

"Yes, it was lovely of your family to invite us".

"Kim, why don't you show Erimentha your room?" Mrs Barton suggests.

"Of course. Do you two want to come up as well?" she says to Beth and another girl I don't recognise.

Her mother gives her an approving nod and the four of us stroll upstairs along hallways of immaculate cream carpets. Kimberly's pumps leave a trail of grassy damp on the floor and I wonder how her family has managed to keep the floor so clean.

"Does your Mum let you wear your shoes upstairs?" I ask tentatively, not wanting to start an argument but knowing that it will prevent one once everybody has left.

"Who are you? Her Mum?" Beth laughs.

"Actually, I'd say she's acting like more of a grandma," the other girl says, looking my outfit up and down and giggling.

"What are you talking about, Gia?" Kimberly says. "I *love* this look. I saw one of those skirts in 'Unpopular and Proud' and wanted to get it but it was just too cheap".

She smiles at me — a white toothy smile which doesn't extend to those cold, blue irises — and then turns back to her friends, laughing at some silly inside joke from earlier. Rather than eavesdrop, I examine the pictures framing the walls. Kimberly's eyes smile from behind the glass in photographs of her and her sister holding turtles, jumping on bouncy castles and playing on empty beaches. They both look a lot happier than the two girls I have become acquainted with.

"Stop staring," Kimberly says. "I know that *you* have no fun but that doesn't give you the right to go looking in on other people's lives. Mum said to show you my room so that's what I'm doing. Do you think I wanted you to come today? Who wants to be associated with Pick-me Parker?"

I find myself looking down at the floor. At her dirty shoes.

With all things considered, I'm not surprised to find that her room is messy. There is a heap of worn clothes next to the laundry basket and her dressing table is strewn with far more makeup than an eleven year old needs. She picks up a tube of lipstick and applies it gingerly to her lips.

"You know, most lipsticks are made from whale blubber?" I say, ready to recount the unethical history of the cosmetics industry, but she holds up her hand to silence me before I have a chance. She walks towards me, standing so that her face is just centimetres from mine and rolling the tube of lipstick between her thumb and forefinger.

"No facts in my house, Erimentha," she whispers.

She looks at me intently for a few seconds and then draws a thick, bulbous line of magneta wax across my left cheek, pressing so hard that the skin distorts upwards and stings.

"Ew. It's got Parker germs all over it", she scrunches up her nose and drops it into the bin. "Thanks for ruining my favourite lipstick".

Beth takes out her phone laughing and I hear the signature iPhone camera click.

"What shall I caption it?"

"Maybe just her name?"

"Or 'avoid this girl at all costs', that might be funnier?"

"Caption this for what, sorry?"

I don't have a phone yet, let alone any social media, and whilst I have read a few articles about the popularity of such networks — learning that, for example, that Facebook has over twenty-five million users! — I am not entirely sure how the sites work in practise.

"Instagram, duh," Beth says rolling her eyes.

"Instagram?" I repeat. "But I haven't given consent for this photograph to be shared?"

"I have a private account".

"Not only that," I continue, "but you have to be at least thirteen to legally have an account. You're breaking the law either way".

I realise that Gia has been filming my little speech and I put my hand over the camera's eye.

"Enough!" Kimberly warns and I immediately subside, internally disappointed at how easily she manages to stop me.

"Sorry" I say involuntarily, not recognising the sound of my own voice. "But hopefully you can turn the other cheek and we can maybe even be friends".

Pastor Michael's sermon rings clear in my ears.

"Sure, Erimentha," she smiles. "Could you sit down on my dressing table chair for a minute?"

Her sickly sweet words dissipate over the bedroom, getting stuck in that repulsive pile of clothes. Beth and Gia help me to the table as if I am suffering with acute arthritis. Beth holds her hands over my eyes and I can smell chocolate on them. I wonder when she last washed them and fight against my gag reflex. I hear the ding of recorded video but the girls are otherwise quiet. I fight against Beth but her and Gia hold me where I am. I can hear a flock of passing carrion crows, wings flapping like rainfall and caws echoing across the Cornish fields. Then I feel something rough on the back of my neck and hear a snip.

Beth removes her hands, doubling over in her laughter and I quickly feel the back of my scalp. There's a chunk missing. I've always kept my hair exactly the same length all of the way around and this loss of order makes me feel sick.

"Don't worry, Erimentha," Kimberly says. "You can't see any difference from the back. Your parents won't notice".

She's already determined that I won't be telling them then. I know that they'd only worry if I did. I am strong enough to deal with this by myself.

95

"We only needed a bit of hair for a voodoo doll we're making".

"Voodoo dolls don't work," I say stoutly.

I've read about them and the only reason that they have become so prominent in the Vodou religion is because of tourism. In New Orleans, the dolls are only really sold to make money. Logically, I shouldn't be afraid of them but I still find that my teeth are chattering. I leave the room quickly and hurry downstairs to find Nathan. He's playing cars with another little boy and Ella is reading on the sofa. I sit down next to her and take out my book as well. I see her smile out from the corner of my eye.

15

I tie my hair into a high ponytail and hold it up to inspect the damage. Kimberly was right: you can't see it when my hair is down, but the ugly tuft is more than evident when I put it up. It juts out like a compound fracture. I hear Mum knock on the door and quickly pull at the hair band, catching a loop of hair painfully which requires an incredible yank. The hair falls like a veil over my shoulders, soundlessly covering the events of the day.

"I'm just finishing washing my face," I say shakily, nearly knocking over the jug as I pick up my flannel again. I've already cleaned my face but a cover-up story is unfortunately now necessary.

"Did you have a nice time today? It was a shame about the weather — I don't know how Grace stayed so calm with all things considered. I know I would have been beside myself with stress!"

"Yes, it was good," I say unconvincingly, climbing into bed.

"You're not going to sleep in plaits? That's new!"

I nod vaguely and pull the covers up to my neck. The sheets are cool against my feet and I move them around to keep warm.

"I feel like we need to return the invite sometime. Maybe we could host our own inside barbecue. Invite the McCloud family as well?"

"I don't know if Kimberly and Juliet would get on".

"Well, we'll think about it".

She kisses me on my forehead. Her lips are damp with the smell of toothpaste.

"Good night, Bumblebee".

***

I take my seat the next morning without meeting Kimberly's eye, leaning over *Much Ado About Nothing* and mouthing Shakespeare's crafted words. The Year Seven chatter makes it difficult to concentrate and I feel someone tugging at my hair, pulling it up so that you can clearly see the back of my neck.

"Looks amazing," Izzy giggles. "You should thank them for their excellent hairdressing skills!"

I can hear the three of them whispering and laughing but decide not to respond. After the barbecue, I read through a few bullying self-help websites (even though I am *not* being bullied) and the number one piece of advice is to ignore it. My tears are quickly absorbed by the open page of my book. It's like when you pour a bucket of water on damp sand at the beach — it will darken but the water soon seeps far below, quickly restoring the colour of the sand.

"Oh Erimentha, it's not like you to ignore us," Kimberly says in feigned confusion. "You're usually *so* opinionated".

Izzy goes to touch my hair again but the door opens and she quickly drops her hand, scampering back to her own seat. Mr Aldridge's entrance temporarily silences my peers but, when he doesn't say anything, their chatter is restored. He sits down at his desk to organise a few papers and I return to *Mansfield Park*.

"How was your weekend, Erimentha?" he asks from across the desk, still shuffling folders and plastic wallets.

"It was wonderful thank you," I say with partial honesty. "How was yours?"

He replies with a similarly vague comment and I flick the pages of my book with my right thumb to release my nervous energy. It has been said that fidgeting can actually reduce stress.

"Were those girls bothering you when I came in just now?"

I shake my head rigorously and try to sound convincing.

"Oh no, it was just playful banter. You know, the sort you can expect between eleven-year-olds! Kimberly and I are actually family friends — I was even invited round to her house yesterday afternoon".

I choose my words carefully, not wanting to directly lie to my form tutor.

"Oh that's good then," he says, looking visibly more relaxed. "Have you thought anymore about who might have sent the emails?"

I shake my head but Mr Aldridge does not look convinced. Before he can press the matter, I retrieve the History Timeline from my bag, having finished it on Saturday morning. He says that it is fantastic, and even gives me three housepoints, and asks if I want to help him clip it up at first break. I agree with a wide smile and leave for first period with a comforting circle of pride in my stomach, but my optimism cracks when I unpack my bag. There is a note lying on top of my neatly arranged schoolbooks:

A history timeline? That's a new low even for you.

I fold it neatly in two and pop it in the back pocket of my folder, ignoring their sniggers.

***

* * *

Mum hasn't managed to book me in for a later tennis slot yet so I don't attend this week. I email Lindsay and Juliet to ask how it went but they must be busy because they don't respond. I keep my email browser open, waiting for the 'ping' of a reply — perhaps Juliet will even ask whether we can call each other on the home phone. I am half-distracted from my homework in this optimistic daze as I contemplate the prospect of spending time with girls who do not despise me.

Mum asks if I want to go food shopping but I shake my head now that I know this is where Kimberly's family shops. I'm actually rather fond of food shopping — I am always allowed to choose a magazine and, recently, I have really enjoyed browsing their selection of autumn snacks.

"I'll pick you up some gingerbread men," Mum says, as though reading my mind.

16

On Wednesday, we make felt in Textiles and, as is customary, I am rather ahead of my classmates. Whilst most are still pulling apart the raw wool, I am spraying mine with soapy water to bind the fibres. I've mixed it with an orange dye which barely tinges the grey wool.

"Oh can I have a go?" Kimberly asks, already snatching the bottle from me.

"Well, I'm not actually finished yet, Kimberly, so I think you're going to have to wait a few minutes. I shouldn't take too long".

"But I need it now and *sharing is caring*," she says with a sickly sweet smile.

She examines the bottle, peering through the frosted plastic.

"What colour even is this?"

"It's meant to be carrot orange, but it looks more peach on the felt," I say with a small giggle.

"Peach is a boring colour", she says, resting her hand on the bottle's lever and aiming the nozzle at my neatly ironed shirt collar. For a second I just stare blankly, unable to comprehend the hatred in those icy eyes. Then she pushes down furiously on the lever, as though counting how many times she can press it in a minute. A broken stream of rich orange flies in an arch between us and the dye seeps through the cotton of my shirt like blood from a wound. She stops and directs the nozzle at my face, holding it so close that it is blurry: light focused behind the retina. I instinctively bring up my hands to shield my face.

"Are you scared that I'll press it?"

I answer with a hurried shake of the head but am reluctant to expose my face again.

"You obviously are. You're literally cowering".

"I'm not," I say, forcing my hands down.

"If you admit that you are, I won't spray you," she says reasonably. "If you lie... well, you're meant to punish bad behaviour, right?"

My thoughts stutter for a few seconds. What am I supposed to do? Which option could possibly restore my dignity? If I tell her that I am scared, I will show myself as weak. If I refuse, well, my face will be stained orange. Even ignoring her, as all of the websites suggest, will not work in my favour this time. I imagine having to explain my dripping face to the class and how embarrassing it will be when people stare at me in the corridors. It is difficult to account for a painted face when you're not at a carnival and I expect that Mr Aldridge will ask questions. I was lucky on Monday but if I turn up to form in this spray-bottle induced state, I will surely not be let off so lightly.

"I'm waiting," Kimberly says, the contraption still hovering in front of my eyes.

"I'm scared of you".

She lowers the bottle and her smile radiates satisfaction.

"Good choice. Now, let's get you cleaned up," she says, motioning to my shirt. "Mr Grimes, Erimentha has had a bit of an accident with the dye. She was trying to refill the bottle and it just went *everywhere*".

She speaks loudly and my class looks bemused at my stained blouse. Mr Grimes looks irritated and runs his hand through his hair.

"How could you be so careless, Erimentha", he sighs. "You better go to the toilet to get yourself cleaned up".

"I can help her?" Kimberly suggests and Mr Grimes agrees indifferently.

I walk ahead of her, furiously, trying not to think too deeply about what I have just said. She *knows* that she can control me now and I don't doubt that she will make use this newly-enforced power. I try to pity her willingness to hurt me, but cannot quite bring myself to do it. Even if she were to apologise right now, I fear that I would be unable to "turn the other cheek," as Pastor Michael told us to on Sunday.

The bathroom is empty and she is blocking the door. I am trapped. She dutifully collects some paper towels from the dispenser and dabs delicately at the cotton shirt.

"Hopefully it will come out. My Mum would be *so* angry if I accidentally spilled paint all down *my* uniform".

"It probably won't. The label said the dye was permanent," I say through gritted teeth.

"Oh no. What will you tell her then?"

"That there was an incident in Textiles".

"Hmm... And you think that she'll leave it at that. What will you say when she asks for specifics?"

"That somebody spilled the dye".

"Now, that's really not good enough, Erimentha. She might think that it was done on purpose and that wouldn't be good now, would it? She might think you were being... bullied or something crazy".

"Well, I'd make sure that she didn't think that".

"I think I'd rather you said that *you* spilled the dye".

"I don't really like to lie, Kimberly," I say shivering slightly.

She picks at her jumper cuff and I see that she has threaded a needle through the green fibres. She holds it up.

"Perhaps I didn't make myself clear," she says slowly. "You are going to lie if somebody asks you".

Yes, I occasionally *withhold* the truth but I could never lie directly to somebody, especially not Mum. I am not prepared to let my morals slip, no matter the consequences and so I simply shake my head.

Before I have a chance to move away, she has grabbed my wrist sharply. My carpal bone aches against her strong hands.

"Don't say no to me Erimentha," she whispers, so quietly that I would not have heard her were there anybody else in the room. She's that I can feel the warmth of her breath.

She takes the needle and hovers it over the inside of my arm, tracing the skin in mid-air as though deciding the best point of contact. Then she lowers it: carefully and deliberately. The tip of the needle presses so hard against the sallow epithelial tissue that a depression forms in the skin. Applying the same pressure, she moves down my arm, leaving a trail of white and I watch quietly. She pauses when she reaches my central forearm, her eyes boring into my forehead, and mine focused on the needle: mesmerised. She pushes down. Hard. It pierces the skin and a bead of blood swells from the pinprick, growing to the the size of a pea before trickling down towards the crease of my elbow. She washes the needle under the tap and threads it back through her jumper as I nurse the small wound with my mouth, wincing at the metallic crimson on my tongue. It doesn't take too long to stop he bleeding and it doesn't even hurt that much. I am just finding it tricky to come to terms with the incessant hatred of the girl beside me.

"Let's go back to the classroom now," she says as though nothing at all has happened.

I change into my spare uniform at lunch and throw away

the damaged shirt, knowing that this is the only way to avoid any questions from Mum.

***

Now that Kimberly knows I'm scared of her, I know there's not really any point in pretending otherwise. I start bypassing them in the corridors, and my answers in class lack any enthusiasm. I'm so worried they'll do something else — something my teachers, peers and parents will find out about — that I do everything I can not to provoke them. And so no-one notices that something is wrong, even when I my voice starts to lose its confident tinge. I start spending every lunchtime in the library — with Ella — and it's always lovely to see the little smile on her face when I join her. Despite my lack of friends, I can never help but return the gesture. We sit on adjacent armchairs and a few times she has even asked me the meanings of words. I suggest she kept a Book of New Words, just like I do, and the very next day I see a baby blue notepad on her lap.

On Thursday, Kimberly and Izzy pass me horrid notes all through Geography class.

Please leave Lady Nightingale's.

Not even June likes you...

What's it like having no-one but teachers as your friends?

I slip them into the pocket at the back of my folder, not wanting anybody to find them, and rush off to the library as soon as the bell rings. I hope to find a book about the Titanic. When I enter, Ms Athena ushers me over to her desk looking serious.

"Ella is very upset but I don't know why. She came in in tears and has been wiping them away ever since. I was hoping that you could maybe talk with her?"

Of course I give her my word, and walk tentatively towards the shaking figure in the armchair. She is sucking on the tip of her thumb as she reads and the tears are streaming down her cheeks, staining them pink. Her breaths are broken and stutter like trees in a midnight breeze against your windowpane.

"Ella?" I say softly. "What happened?"

Her eyes are almost completely closed because of the tears and I wonder how she has been reading. She doesn't smile when she looks up but her crying ceases temporarily. She manages a quick hello but even this gets swallowed in a sob.

"Can you come with me to the toilet, Ella?" I ask gently, offering my hand. "Let's see if we can get you cleaned up".

She doesn't say anything but takes my hand. Her fingertips are cold.

"Why don't you stand slightly behind me? That way nobody will see that you're crying".

She nods and hangs a step behind my own, still clasping tightly to my hand. We pass a good dozen people but nobody comments on Ella's state. It doesn't seem that anybody even realises. The toilets are thankfully empty and I take a few paper towels from the dispenser, trying not to think about the last time I was alone in a bathroom with a Barton sister. I shake it from my mind. Ella's worries are much more important than my own.

"Now, what's wrong, Ella?" I ask once her tears have been cleared up a little bit.

Still breathing quite quickly, she explains that two girls in her class are being really rather horrid to her. Initially, they were simply leaving her out but, this morning, one of them took her book and started throwing it around the classroom.

"They said I had no friends," she snivels.

"Well, that's not true," I say, my heart breaking at those

solemn, darkened eyes. "Because us two are friends".

She looks up from under her fringe and I think that she smiles but her lips are trembling too much for me to be completely sure.

"I think that we should tell your teacher, Ella," I suggest carefully.

She flinches as though I have gone to hit her and then hangs her head so low that her chin is almost touching her shirt collar. She shuffles her feet nervously.

"What about you?" she squeaks.

"What about me?" I ask, suddenly very aware of the chatter of girls in the corridor.

"Well, aren't you getting bullied, Erimentha?"

My epiglottis seizes up, as though I have swallowed a tablet without water. Ella seems to gain confidence from my silence and slowly averts her eyes from the floor. She walks behind me and peels something from the back of my blazer, then hands me the torn sheet of lined paper: *This girl has no friends. Avoid at all costs!* There are pieces of black lint stuck to the sellotape.

"Maybe we could tell together?"

She looks hopeful and, as an older student, I suppose I should take heed of her suggestion: be a good example. Instead I shake my head. If the two of us speak to a teacher, Ella will know that it's her sister who is being mean to me.

"Ella, mine isn't bullying. At least not in the same way as yours. Besides, I am quite a bit older than you and can cope with this unkindness by myself," I try to say assertively. "But I do want you to speak with your form tutor. In fact, I am happy to come with you right now?"

Ella looks apprehensive and nibbles on the nail of her left ring finger.

"I don't want you to tell, Erimentha," she says anxiously. "I think I can cope with it too. I don't think that they'll do anything else. It was just a one-time thing".

I bite my lip and crinkle my brow. I know I really should help Ella get this sorted but I equally know how upset *I* would have been if Simone had told Mr Aldridge. Besides, it would be wrong to report the incident as bullying if this was the first time anything had happened — when I searched for the definition, it was made clear that bullying was *repetitive*. I half-heartedly agree not to tell but insist that she lets me know if anything else happens. It's only when we are sitting back in the library, once more engaged in our reading, that I begin to question whether my situation has actually become a form of bullying.

17

When I walk in for afternoon registration, I see that my satchel has been ransacked. The bag is upturned, the strap hanging haphazardly, and the desk scattered with torn exercise books, scrunched up pieces of paper and stray pens. The room is thankfully empty and I hurry to clear everything away before Mr Aldridge comes in. I smooth out the papers and slide them in the front of my folder, knowing that even organisation will have to wait this time. I stash my books neatly inside of my bag, trying not to bend them further. Most of my stationery has gone missing. Since the ink incident in Geography last week, I have been using my spare pencil case but even this is gone now. I search the classroom, just in case it has been flung beneath the radiator, but am without luck. I can't find all but one of my pencils and my set of coloured fine-liners is nowhere to be seen. By the time June comes in, everything has been tidied up and I am sorting through stray pieces of paper, trying to find their proper homes. She looks uncomfortable and I say hello in what I hope to be a cheerful voice. She turns back on herself awkwardly, incoherently murmuring that she has to see a teacher. I stay sat in the classroom, looking after the frazzled girl I had once considered a friend.

* * *

***

Of course, I have spare stationery but I've lost my favourite set of pastel highlighters and so ask Mum if we can go stationery shopping on Saturday afternoon. Using a list which I composed a couple of months ago, I repack my school satchel for the trip.

Things to bring on a shopping trip:
* *A purse (because without it, shopping is impossible)*
* *A book (you never know when you might need it)*
* *My receipt book (seeing as it is important to keep a track of all purchases)*
* *A lip balm (parched lips will never do)*
* *An umbrella (you can never discount the possibility of rain in England)*
* *Suncream (as we have already established, British weather is rather unpredictable)*
* *A hand sanitiser (money carries lots of germs)*
* *Hand cream (hand sanitiser can dry out your hands)*
* *A canvas book bag (after all, five trillion plastic bags are used each year!)*
* *Post-It notes and a pen (when don't you need them?)*
* *The Book of Reminders (obviously)*

On Friday night, I lay out a midnight blue velvet skirt, white cable-knit jumper and some comfortable brown boots and Mum agrees to wear something similar. I do love it when we colour-coordinate. When I was a lot younger, Mum bought us matching yellow dresses for church and I delighted at the sense of order that it brought — I wanted us to wear them everyday and was terribly dismayed when I eventually outgrew it. I believe that Mum kept hers but she doesn't wear it anymore, feeling guilty that she, unlike me, still has access to the much-loved dress. It's cold and I slip on my beige duffle coat and a simple black scarf but even then I have to hold my chest with both hands to prevent the icy chill from spreading too far.

"Do you know what the coldest temperature ever measured was? At the Vostok Station in East Antarctica?" I shiver to Mum. "How cold do you suppose it was?"

"Hmm... minus one hundred degrees Celsius?" Mum guesses and I feel a bit disheartened. I asked her this question for the shock factor but her guess is *lower* than the actual answer.

"No, it was actually minus eighty-nine degrees," I say.

"And then you've got us two who are shivering away on this warm four degrees Celsius day!".

I giggle a little bit too, wondering how the two of us would fare as extreme tourists visiting the Antarctic Peninsula. As though reading my mind, she asks me if I'd ever visit Antarctica.

"Well it would be interesting, of course, but I don't really think that tourists should be visiting at all. You know, the petrol from the boats is detrimental to the krill population? I'd only ever visit if I was there doing something good. Like saving the krill or helping the penguins".

Mum laughs as she pushes open the door to Paperchase.

"I can't think of anything worse. Cold weather is just depressing, Erimentha," she says. "I really don't know why you love it so much".

"But the colours of autumn are just *so* beautiful — when October arrives, it is as though a homemade quilt has been laid across the countryside for the hibernating animals," I say dreamily. "And you must admit that it's just wonderful snuggling up inside under blankets while the window panes grow frosty".

Mum admits her agreement as I examine a star-speckled pencil case.

"Mind you, I do love the clear summer evenings where the stars are so bright that it's as though you can trace the constellations with your fingertips. Perhaps we could draw out a map of the night sky together?"

"Oh, I don't know about that — it's not really my thing — but I'll get you some black craft paper now so that you can do it tomorrow after church?"

I agree heartily and dash off to find the paper. When I return, an elderly lady, not much older than Grandmama, is talking with Mum.

"I just wanted to commend you for the raising of such a well-behaved and charming daughter," I overhear. "My grandchildren are forever commenting on the latest phones and technology and it's not every day that you see such a grateful and content little girl".

She sees me approaching and smiles warmly before turning away.

After visiting every stationery shop in the shopping centre, we find a quaint deli where Mum orders a black coffee and I get a hot chocolate. Knowing that it will otherwise scald my tongue, I ask for it to be topped up with cold water and, sure enough, I take my first sip without any damage to my taste buds. Mum is not quite so lucky.

"Why didn't I follow your example?" she exclaims, holding her cool finger against her scalded tongue.

The cafe serves miniature jam pots with their cream teas and I ask the lady at the counter whether I could have some to take home. I fancy that they will make excellent candle holders. She checks with her supervisor but neither one thinks this a problem and I am given a small cardboard box with a seven jars. We collect some beeswax and wicks from the home goods market before heading home.

* * *

***

It's a chilly evening and I bundle up in a warm turtle neck and jumper. Despite the cold, the blustery winds have calmed and the near-naked trees do not shiver against the night. I have made a cocoon on the patio bench, snuggled up under such a multitude of blankets and cushions that I cannot feel the cool September air. I am wearing gloves which makes it difficult to turn the pages of my book and I eventually take them off, frustrated. Mum and I spent the afternoon making candles and I have used them to form a fairy ring of light around me. They glow against the dark, faded denim of the sky, and soft orange light cascades from the jam jars, sending a warming signal through the mist. I snuggle up closer to the cushions, my nose covered by a blanket. It is damp and hot and would be uncomfortable were it not so chilly. They say that this is one of the coldest Septembers on record and I smile at this factoid. Whilst my family and peers have not stopped short of complaining of this 'typical British weather', I am truly thrilled. After all, I can think of no better way to be spending a Saturday night. Protected by this circle of lights, an arabesque against the cold, the girls at Lady Nightingale's cannot hurt me.

18

We are learning about refraction in science and Mrs Stafford puts us into pairs. She doesn't think too much of her decision, assuming that any two girls can learn to get along, and whilst I am certainly willing to turn over a new leaf, Beth is not quite so open. When our names are read out, she sighs hyperbolically and a few people whisper their condolences from across the room. They watch my reaction from the corners of their eyes. It doesn't bother me — I suppose I have calloused to this unpleasantness — but my heart falls when I see that June is giggling too.

Beth slams her books down on the desk surface, muttering something about the injustice of the whole situation.

"All right, we should go get all of the apparatus first", I try to say cheerfully.

She looks over to Izzy, rolling her eyes and giggling.

"Why don't *you* do it?" she suggests.

I hold her gaze for a few seconds, my eyes steady and controlled, hers dull and brown. But when a few of her friends start to laugh, I know it's not worth it. I clench my teeth and write a quick Post-It note list of the required equipment, my low ponytail swinging as I turn. There's quite a lot to gather up and I have to make two trips, my heart beating with furious anger the whole time. Beth is talking to a group of girls on the other side of the classroom and when she leans in to whisper something, they look around round at me in unison. I hold my head high and ignore my stinging eyes.

"Beth, we really must get on with the practical," I say, my teeth still clenched.

"Is anyone willing to swap partners? I don't think I can physically stand Pick-Me Parker's presence for a whole hour!" she says loudly, looking around "Try and put yourself in my shoes, guys".

I purse my lips and try to keep my face level with hers, which is tricky because she is a couple of inches taller than me. Mind you, her poor posture does make her rather a lot shorter.

"It's not an hour — Mrs Stafford said it was only a thirty minute practical," I say tightly.

"Aha, look at her with her nose stuck in the air. You really do think you're better than everyone don't you Erimentha?" one girl, Ally, laughs. "No wonder June ditched you. I probably would have too if I'd been lumbered with you on the first day".

"Ally, you're not going to tell her, are you?" another girl gasps and I look between the two sharply. Funnily enough, I realise I'd much rather they insulted me directly than talked about behind my back.

"What's this you were going to tell me?" I say, a little more softly this time.

"Oh nothing. It's not important," Beth grins. "Shall we get on with the practical then?"

I nod impassively and purposefully arrange the apparatus as is specified on the board.

"Let's try the plastic straw first," I suggest. "Do you want to put it in?"

She drops it into the bowl of water and so floats sideways on top. I reposition it so that it is half-in and half-out, just as the diagram specifies.

"It truly is fascinating, isn't it Beth? I remember wondering why the straw appeared to bend in my glass at a restaurant once but I didn't remember to research it! I've heard of reflection and diffraction but refraction is a totally new term for me".

I am so enthused by the learning that I temporarily forget we're not friends. She has probably been rolling her eyes the whole way through my little speech and I bet all of my peers have been listening. I fall silent at this thought.

"Pretty cool," Beth smiles passive aggressively.

She wanders off again and, rather than object, I continue with the experiment, internally curious as to why Mrs Stafford has not yet commented on Beth's absence. Ordinary, she jumps at the slightest indication of misbehaviour. I look around quickly, not making eye-contact with the sniggering girls to my left, and realise that she is not here. I frown and turn back to the water. The slight slant of the room means that the meniscus does not sit level. It makes my stomach turn. I see Beth whisper a last, and invariably snide, remark to her friends before sauntering back over.

"Sorry Erimentha, would you mind if I copy your notes?" She says, twirling a strand of hair around her finger.

I tense my shoulders slightly, "But that would dismiss the whole point of doing a practical..."

I never let anyone copy. I don't see the point. Remarkably, Beth accepts this and forces a smile, "Of course, Erim. How could I be so silly? Would you mind if I have a go?"

She pushes me to the side so that she stands over the bowl and reaches for the three damp marbles, dropping them in one by one — she then bends down with interest, "Oh, look at that! It's so cool!".

She ponders for a moment.

"What other objects could demonstrate refraction?" she wonders aloud, tapping a perfectly manicured fingernail against her front tooth.

She gasps, as though a magnificent idea has come to her.

"What do you think paper would do?" She asks excitedly.

She searches purposefully through the equipment on the desk then holds up something triumphantly: my three page, handwritten extension essay on the existence of photons.

I go to stop her but she shoves me painfully into the desk behind. I search for Mrs Stafford but she hasn't returned.

Beth lays the paper on the water's surface and it floats momentarily, like a feather on a frozen pond. She pushes lightly upon the centre and three droplets form, rounded like paperweights and temporarily stationary. The moment bursts and water dribbles across the page, leaving a strand of diluted ink. Beth clutches my wrist and forces my hand down upon the one hundred percent recycled paper, fully submerging the assignment until nothing, save a pencil-drawn diagram and a blur of blue, remains.

"You're so careless, Erimentha," she says sweetly. "Fancy ruining your own piece of homework".

***

I retire to the library with heavy eyelids and a headache and choose a particularly comforting novel: *Harry Potter and The Goblet of Fire*, my favourite in the series. I collapse into the story, swimming in the Black Lake and pretending that I too have a friend I can rescue. Surprisingly, I haven't heard from Juliet since our tennis lesson at the beginning of term. I expect that her and Lindsay are simply too preoccupied with their new schools to be thinking about me. They probably think I have settled in marvellously — after all, that's what I told them. A schoolbell rings in the distance and I can hear Ms Athena pattering around the library, light on her feet so as not to disturb the girls who are studying. Ella walk in, looking especially solemn, but her eyes grow bright, crinkling like book pages when she sees me.

"Hallo Erimentha," she says. "I do hope that you had a smashing weekend!".

"I did indeed — it was marvellous!" I reply, "Did you by any chance take up my Malory Towers book recommendation over the weekend?"

"Yes, I did actually," she laughs. "I'm trying to talk just like them, you know".

I giggle as well, remembering how my own mannerisms had changed after reading the series. We stifle our laughter so as not to attract the attention of the librarian and I realise that I have indeed found a friend here. Yes, she is an entire two years younger than myself but that's hardly important. How wonderful it would be if the two of us were in the same form. Not only would I have a friend to sit with, but Kimberly wouldn't dare torment me in the presence of her sister.

"Ella, all jokes aside, how are you?" I ask. It takes the girl a few seconds to regain her composure, she is laughing so hard.

"Mmm," she hums vaguely. "It's been fine".

I narrow my eyes at her, but not sternly.

"This morning was just a simple misunderstanding," she says quickly, averting her gaze. "They snapped my ruler but I'm pretty sure it was an accident".

"And how did they get your ruler?" I ask gently.

"They took my whole pencil case and were throwing it around, being really silly".

"Did you ask them to stop?"

"Yes, but they probably didn't hear me. You know, they say I'm as quiet as a small, dead mouse".

I've got to admit, Ella does look a bit like a mouse. She has the same long front teeth and pointed nose. Her eyes, however, make all of the difference for they are so large that they could never be compared to the small, beady optics of a rodent. Nonetheless, I suppose that 'mouse' is rather a sweet nickname. Mind you, nobody would particularly like to be referred to as a *dead* mouse. That really is rather nasty.

"That's not nice at all, Ella," I say. "These girls have been horrid to you".

"Well what about you, Erimentha," she says quickly, even fearfully. "What have they done to you this morning?"

I don't say anything, not wanting to lie but equally not wanting to reveal anything incriminating.

"I told you what happened to *me*," she reminds me. "And I promise that you can trust me".

Reluctantly, I recount the events of physics and she gasps, insisting that it is far worse than her own misadventures.

"Erimentha, please let's tell somebody!" she says with a crinkled brow.

"I've told you, Ella, mine isn't anything to worry about — we've already been told that it can be expected in Year Seven. What'ss happening to you, on the other hand, certainly needs to be dealt with and I really do think we should tell a teacher".

"I'm not going to tell unless you do," she says stubbornly and I stand up quickly.

"Okay then. Well, it looks like neither of us are going to say anything," I say, disappointed at how immature I must sound and also at how rude I am being to poor Ella. She hardly needs this right now.

She certainly does look muddled and stands up too, following me out into the corridor.

"I don't mind that we don't tell," she says, sounding panicked. "But please don't be angry with me. I can't lose you as a friend as well. You're the only person in the whole of this school who seems to actually like me and I don't know what I'll do if you hate me. Please, Erimentha".

She starts to cry. Warm, steamy tears. Right there in the middle of the corridor.

A Sixth Former asks Ella what is wrong but she shakes her head loyally and insists that she just needs to talk to 'the kind Year Seven girl over there'. The older girl pats me on the back and gives me an encouraging smile, treating me with kindness that I certainly do not deserve right now. I put my arm around my friend to lead her into the bathroom and only then realise that I'm crying too.

"I'm sorry, Ella," I say, "but I can't tell. You're right — people have been being mean to me and I'm sorry that I wasn't entirely honest with you but I *can't* tell".

Ella stays silent, watching me with those dark eyes which are so different from her older sister's.

"I know that I'm being hypocritical but we need to get it sorted out for *you*", I say. "I can't stand by and watch you being bullied".

"And I can't stand by and watch *you* being bullied," she replies breathlessly.

"Look, Ella. I'm older than you. I know that you're mature for your age but you can't be expected to suffer through these girls' behaviour. No matter what you say, I'm going to go and talk to your form tutor right this instant. I'm just going to have to trust you to not say anything about what is happening to me".

Ella looks down at the floor, tears dribbling down her jumper.

"I know I'm being harsh, Ella. But I care about you too much to let this happen".

I know that she cares about me too — why else would she be so keen to get my unfriendliness sorted? — but I can't let her discover that her own sister is the one bullying me. I hate how obtuse and hypocritical I am being but it can't be helped. I lead Ella to the staff room, knock thrice on the wooden door and ask for her form tutor.

19

I arrive to Physical Education promptly and change before any of my peers arrive. The tennis courts are empty and I run a quick lap of the vicinity, struggling to get warm. The sky is blue but the air is crisp and cold and I shiver underneath my jumper. The sun is watery amongst Byron's "cloudless climes" and warms my scalp as though it were once again August. It is queer that barely a month ago the sun was so hot there was a hose pipe ban; that barely a month ago, I wasn't scared to walk down school corridors by myself. The late September frost means that the court is a little bit slippery and I watch my feet as I jog, careful not to make a spectacle of myself by falling over. I can hear the chatter of eleven-year-olds drifting across the grassy ridge in front of the pitch: meaningless talk of weekend plans and television shows. I can hear Kimberly's distinctively sly voice diffracting around the hill.

"Come on! Hurry up!" Mr Longrich calls. "See here, Miss Parker's waiting for us all already. You really need to practise getting dressed more quickly — it shouldn't be that difficult kids!"

I can see my peers sniggering as he turns my way, his uncovered knees already turning blue in the cold.

"You can have a house point for that speedy changing, Miss," he says loudly, only making the other students giggle more.

He waits until we are all standing in a circle around him, our feet shifting from right to left and our sleeves pulled over our frozen fingertips. Melody's teeth are chattering as she tries to revert her body temperature back to thirty seven degrees Celsius.

"Alright, it's a bit chilly today so we're going to start with a game of Around the World," Our teacher says. "I assume everybody knows how to play".

I agree loudly, my voice momentarily piercing the birdsong. A few of my peers murmur inaudibly and Mr Longrich reluctantly explains the rules. Seven of us gather on one side of the court and the other half stands opposite, still shivering. I am first and my serve, if I do say so myself, is nearly perfect. I guide the ball to June's racket, giving her an easy shot, before hopping around to the back of the queue.

"Oh *I* know how to do it, Mr Longrich, because I am just *so* perfect," Kimberley imitates, making a ridiculous face.

"I am *definitely* better than all of *you*," Ally adds in the same silly voice.

"Listen, I would appreciate it if you didn't mock me," I say quickly, turning away to watch the game.

"Us? Mocking you?" Kimberly says in feigned surprise. "Surely you don't think that we would ever be mean to *you*. I mean, we're practically your best friends".

"I thought I didn't have any friends?"

"Oh yeah, I forgot. You're a loner," Ally laughs, running off to hit the ball.

"She's just kidding," Kimberly says, tapping me on the shoulder in the same way that a friend would.

She hurries off to the centre of the court and returns the ball cleanly, her short ponytail grazing her shoulder as she leans to the right. I haven't been able to wear a ponytail since the day of the barbecue. I receive the next shot: a particularly tricky back-hand and Mr Longrich shouts out his compliments. I catch back up with Kimberly.

"I was just telling Ally that you're *not* a loner. I mean, you are so popular that you even have your own fan page!"

"Fan page?" I question.

"Yeah, someone made this website all about you and how amazing you are. I'll write down the link on one of your prized Post-It notes if you want?"

I gingerly pass her the pad concealed in my skirt pocket, and she quickly jots something down. I return it to my hiding place, not even consulting the hyperlink, my heart beating with furious nerves.

"So now that you're famous, I'm thinking that we could even be *best* friends," Kimberly says, linking her arm tightly around mine, "In fact, we should eat lunch together tomorrow?"

I ease my arm from hers, "No thanks, Kimberly".

"Come on", she says again, her voice sickly sweet.

Mr Longrich congratulates Melody on an excellent return, his voice loud and growling against the wind.

"Yeah come on", Beth adds.

"There's no-one I'd rather be friends with. Honest".

A distant airplane passes overhead and I remember how Nathan and I used to wave to them when we were small. My stomach clenches as Kimberly takes my arm again, her fingernails digging into the skin.

"I don't know what you're doing", I say quietly and steadily, my eyes flitting up to hers. "But can you just leave me alone. Please".

I wait for her to loosen her grip and, when she doesn't, I yank my arm quickly away and turn around to watch June serve. She throws the ball high above her head and hits it before it bounces, her movement smooth. The ball makes a bee-line for Ally's racket and I hear the swish of a tennis racket behind me. For a millisecond, my head feels heavy. Like someone has filled it with paperweights. And I wonder how I've managed to keep this weight propped up on my shoulders. And then everything goes white.

***

I'm still standing but am so dizzy that it feels like I'm about to keel over. I lower myself to the ground, my head throbbing, and feel somebody's arm on my shoulder.

"Has someone gone to get the nurse?" Mr Longrich shouts.

I lay my head down on the tarmac, my eyes scrunched up from the pain, and reach a shaky hand to my head, tenderly tracing the bump on the back of my head.

"Erimentha," somebody says gently. "Erimentha, are you okay?"

"Mum?" I croak.

"Fancy calling her Mum," someone whispers. "How embarrassing".

"No, dearie, it's Sister Lizzie. The school nurse. You've taken a nasty blow to the head. We've just put you down on the tarmac".

The nurse gently pushes my shoulders back to the floor when I make to sit up

"Just stay there for now, Erimentha. I don't want you passing out. Your Mum's been phoned and is going to pick you up and take you to hospital".

"Because I'm concussed," I murmur but it goes unnoticed.

She eases me up and into a wheelchair nearby and I smile as June takes my left arm. She looks awkward but smiles back.

"Now girls, what happened just now?" the nurse asks Ally.

"A&E will need to know".

Ally stutters, searching for an excuse, but it is Kimberly who steps in, surprisingly sounding rather tearful.

"I feel terrible. I completely blame myself. I was bouncing my ball on my racket — you know, trying to see how many times I could do it, and I just completely lost control. The ball went straight into the back of Erimentha's head".

She even goes as far as to feign a large sob and Mr Longrich pats her shoulder comfortingly, assuring her that she needn't feel responsible. The nurse, on the other hand, does not look convinced.

"Erimentha was hit really hard with that tennis ball. I'd be surprised if it were an accident".

Kimberly looks at her nonplussed as Sister Lizzie looks between the two of us. But before she can say anything else, Mr Longrich mouths something her way and, pursing her lips, she reluctantly gives a nod of acknowledgement. She wheels me to the infirmary and June offers to run and collect my things from the changing room.

"It sure is nice that you've got such a kind friend," she says from her computer.

"Yes," I agree, "June can be lovely".

"What about the girl who hit you in the back of the head? Can she be lovely?".

I don't say anything, staring instead at the little scratch on my kneecap where she'd tripped me up yesterday. Sister Lizzie sighs and turns from the computer screen, her swivel chair squeaking.

"I don't know whether that was an accident or not", she says. "But I somehow doubt it".

"I suppose it's easy to lose control of the ball", I say quietly.

"Yes, I suppose it is. But she'd have to have been properly mucking around to have hit you that hard".

"All eleven year olds muck around?"

"Yes, they do", she sighs. "All I'm asking, Erimentha, is whether it's really that difficult to imagine she did this on purpose? Do you and her get on?"

I reposition myself in the chair, not wanting to lie, but neither wanting to tell the truth. If I tell her about Kimberly, Ella will find out and be heartbroken. I can't do that to her.

"I'm best friends with her sister", I say, finally making eye contact, "so I'd be surprised if Kimberly would do something like that to me".

I'm not really lying. After all, it is surprising.

***

Whilst I'm dismayed at having to spend the afternoon in the Accident and Emergency waiting room, I do enjoy observing the patients around me. One middle-aged man seems to have a broken arm — at least that's what I can infer from the deep bruising around the ulna bone. I am tempted to ask but he looks as though he is in rather enough agony as it is and a conversation might not be exactly what he's looking for right now. It's said that chatting can divert your thoughts from an injury; however, when the talk is *about* the injury, I am not sure if this is still quite the case. Luckily for me and my boredom, Mum has brought some bits to while away the time. I keep a 'Emergency Hospital Supply Kit' in a large plastic box in my wardrobe — for incidents just like this. Me being rather careful, I have never made use of it in the past but am glad now that I am so organised. I made it clear to my parents that the box should be taken with them when heading to the hospital.

"It will save you any stress when you arrive," I reasoned.

Erimentha Parker's Emergency Hospital Supply Kit:

* *A spare change of clothes*
* *A pair of pyjamas*
* *Spare underwear*
* *A toothbrush, toothpaste, mouthwash and floss*
* *A hairbrush and hairbands*
* *Peppermint lip balm, soap, hand cream, hand sanitiser and a flannel*
* *'Charlotte, Sometimes' and 'The Origins of Species'*
* *A notepad and pen*

Of course, the box assumes that I will be staying overnight and, seeing as this is only a simple case of concussion, I suppose I must look rather silly with this massive box of goodies. The doctor looks bemused when she sees it but doesn't make a comment and proceeds to check me all over. I am given a pamphlet on concussion, despite already having one printed, and am deemed safe to return home.

"If anything worrying pops up, bring her back," she says.

I thank her and she thanks me, complimentarily telling me that I am one the most medically informed children she's met. She asks if it is my ambition to go into medicine myself but I simply tilt my head to the side.

"I'm not quite sure yet," I say. "Perhaps I will become a doctor but I'm also considering politics, environmental conservation and maybe teaching English".

She smiles at Mum before bidding me farewell. On the way out, I give the man with the broken arm my condolences and say that I hope that he recovers quickly and painlessly. His smile makes me glad to have said it.

20

The next morning, Mum says that I can stay off from school. Ordinarily I would refuse in a heartbeat but today I think about it. Kimberly probably won't be too happy at having gotten into trouble and it's more than likely she'll try something especially horrid today. The rational part of my brain assures me that staying off from school will do nothing to resolve the situation — she'll only postpone her maliciousness for the following day — but I still accept Mum's offer.

"You must feel bad!" Mum laughs. "Do you want some Calpol for your headache?"

I shake my head, "I read that you can become immune to painkillers if you take them too regularly. I'm not feeling *dreadful* and so would rather save them".

Bemused, Mum asks if I want to walk Nathan to school this morning and I agree heartily. Perhaps I will even be able to say a quick hello to Mrs Luton. I bundle up in my beige duffle coat, brown boots and a thick red jumper, crunching the oak leaves underfoot. It's a particularly windy day and with each gust, a host of leaves spiral from the tree tops, pirouetting and twirling before landing in an arabesque on the pavement. In some queer way, it seems a shame to break them.

Nathan and I race to the end of the road, my plait bouncing on my back and my eyes streaming from the cold. He wins and I pat him on the back encouragingly, bending over in my laughter, unable to even pinpoint the source of my sudden joy.

"Did you know—" I begin but Nathan cuts me off.

"No more facts!" he laughs, pushing my shoulder slightly.

I know he's joking but I am painfully reminded of Kimberly's words the weekend before last and fall silent.

"Don't be mean, Nathan," Mum says sharply, noticing my withdrawal. "We love Erimentha's little factoids".

This makes me giggle — Mum's forever telling me how frustrating my constant pursuit of knowledge is. She hyperbolically, but insincerely, groans whenever I start with a signature *'Did you know…?'*.

"I was just going to say that laughter is one of the best natural defences against stress and discomfort".

"Yes, I did know that one actually. A book came out about the whole notion of laughing twenty odd years ago. Instant success. Your Dad and I read it together actually".

Mum studied psychology at university and Dad studied English. They met at York over a particularly strenuous examination season. It sounds terribly romantic and, despite being somewhat critical of the very *idea* of love, I have asked Mum to recount the tale many a time. Nathan usually cringes away, him being a stereotypical eight-year-old boy and all.

The playground is crowded with children when we arrive. My old headmistress is supervising them, berating two particularly tiny girls for their silliness. Mum stays at the gate but urges me to pop in and say hello. I really don't like the idea of standing out. There is something rather unnerving about trawling through a field of children, knowing that you are separate from all of them. I seem to blend in well enough amongst their colourful coats and know that my height could quite easily pass me as a Year Five but am still cautious. Funnily enough, nobody does so much as look at me until my old headmistress catches my eye.

"Oh heavens, Erimentha. What a wonderful surprise," she says. "How are you enjoying your new school? Aren't you at Longrich Grammar?"

"Oh no, I'm at Lady Nightingle's actually and am loving it!"

"Made lots of new friends, I bet!" she exclaims and I nod meekly, forcing a smile.

"I was hoping to talk to Mrs Luton actually, if she's in school that is".

The headmistress agrees absentmindedly, now distracted by a little boy with a grazed knee. She waves a hurried goodbye before heading off to find a plaster. I am tentative in my movements down the corridor. It feels like something of a museum — as though the artwork preserved on the walls was painted centuries ago. I notice a display of sunflowers that my class drew in our art lessons in the summer term of Year Six. I search for mine and Juliet's names and look nostalgically at the names of children who are already beginning to drift into my subconscious. On the last day, I exchanged numbers and addresses with nearly all of them and yet we do not seem to have actually stayed in contact. It seems a shame. After all, we spent four years at St. Agnes's Primary School together. My recollective daze is broken by a gentle voice.

"Erimentha? Oh, my lovely, how fantastic to see you".

I turn around to see Mrs Luton. Nothing about her seems to have changed. She holds her hands together in front of her stomach and her head is tilted to the left, a smile peeking out from the corner of her lips. Even her clothes are the same. She's wearing her signature purple skirt with a thick khaki cardigan. Her over-sized glasses and slight wrinkles establish her as a maternal figure. She's the kind of teacher that I would have felt comfortable telling anything.

"Mrs Luton. It's wonderful to see you too!" I say.

"What are you doing here though?" she asks, tilting her head even further towards her shoulder.

"Well, I was hit in the head by a tennis ball yesterday so Mum thought it best to keep me off. I thought it would be a nice idea to walk Nathan to school. You know, for old-time's sake".

She nods empathetically, asking me about Lady Nightingale's and how I am enjoying it. I half-heartedly tell her that it is great, glancing back at the sunflower display so as not to make eye-contact. She narrows her eyes slightly, her front teeth nibbling on the inside of her lip.

"Are you really enjoying it, Erimentha?"

My breath catches in the back of my throat and I nod uncertainly. She looks at me for a long moment, flitting between both eyes just like Mum does.

"Something's not right, my lovely. Why don't you tell me what?".

I hold her gaze but my thoughts whirl like the October leaves outside. Tellings Mrs Luton might not actually be too bad an idea. After all, she doesn't know Kimberly and so the chances are that Ella will never find out. Then again, she might tell Mum and, even if Mrs Luton *doesn't* say anything, I'll have admitted that I'm weak. Yes, I'm being treated less than fairly but I have read that the most important thing is that the victim does not manifest their vulnerability and me telling a teacher does just this.

"Well, there has been *some* unkindness, I've got to admit," I say, trying not to exemplify the situation.

"What like?"

"Oh, you know, just typical Year Seven behaviour," I say

132

vaguely.

The bell rings and Mrs Luton glances over her shoulder.

"I really can't stay for very long, Erimentha. I'll need to get to my class but I want you to promise me that you'll do your best to get this sorted. You don't deserve to be treated like this, my lovely, and I don't want for these mean girls to take away your smile and love for learning. You're a sensible girl and I trust you to make the right decision. I think you should tell your parents or maybe a teacher at your new school? I'm sure you have some adults you can trust to get this resolved".

I nod and wave goodbye as the morning tide of chattering Year Six girls beats against the carpeted corridor shore. I am regretting having said anything but still contemplate her suggestion. Debasish Mridha insists that we "keep the window of the mind open to let the fresh thoughts come in like fresh air" (a quote which I have pinned to my bedroom door). Without an open mind, after all, we have no chance of progress.

21

The postman has been by the time we arrive back home and I am delighted to find a letter from Grandmama. She usually writes me something the Saturday that I visit and so it's a surprise for it to have come so late. I make myself a large mug of jasmine tea before sitting down in my armchair to read it.

Dear Erimentha,

As always, thank you for your lovely letter. I can imagine why you were excited to start at Lady Nightingale's. I recently realised that the lady next door to me, Meredith, has a granddaughter there called Elizabeth. Seeing as she's in the year above you, I doubt that you two are acquainted but I always feel that coincidences should be documented! In answer to your question, yes, I was nervous for my first day of Year Seven. Things were arguably even worse in my case, however, because not only was I moving into a completely new school environment but it was my first time at boarding school. At your age I only spoke French (well, and a little bit of Portuguese) and my parents were insistent on me becoming fluent in English, them never having grasped the language themselves. So I was shipped off to England with the promise I would only see them once a year. The first few weeks were less than favourable and I made not a single friend, principally because nobody could understand me. It was a difficult time, and would have been for anybody. I felt totally alone; it was as though not a single person cared about me. Then I met a little girl called Chloe who, by some marvellous coincidence, was from Albertville in Southern France. Her mother was born in London and she spoke English well but was embarrassed by her French accent, meaning she was reluctant to raise her voice in class. So absorbed in my own worries, I paid little attention to the girl, not even having realised that she and I shared a mother tongue. One Saturday we were in the school library whilst a few ventured down to the village shops. I rarely glanced up from my own page (why would you, after all?), but this day, after having read a particularly beautiful chapter, I did and my gaze fell upon Chloe's own novel: 'Le Petit Prince'. In French, I asked her how she was finding it and she, surprised herself, tentatively, in her native tongue, agreed that it was lovely. Chloe and I remained the closest friends for the remainder of our time at school. I know that you have heard this story countless times before, Erimentha, but I have been thinking a lot about what you told me last Saturday. Even though you might currently feel isolated at school, remember that you can find friends: remember that there are people similar to you. All you have to do is look up.

All of my love,
Grandmama

After reading through it a few times, I stick the letter to the inside of my wardrobe door. The corners of the paper protrude slightly, like bubblegum, so I use my forefinger to smooth down the imperfections. I admire the effortless calligraphy of my Grandmother. Her handwriting has always been gorgeous, ever since she was a little girl. She showed me one of her nine-year-old self's composition books, filled with the most delicate and graceful words. Each one sat perfectly on the line and looped extravagantly across the paper, though not in the forced manner of most children.

I sit down at my desk and take out a piece of faux-parchment paper to compose a list. In John Agard's 'Book', I read that real parchment was actually the product of dried animal skin and since then I have always made sure to specify that my parchment is *fake!* I try my best to reticulate Grandmama's handwriting.

People at Lady Nightingale's who are similar to Erimentha Parker:

Ella Barton (whilst she is considerably younger than myself, the two of us really do have a lot in common. Not only do we both love books, but we also find refuge in the library and have had to cope with unkindness).

Simone Randolph (she clearly loves Geography, something that I am equally infatuated with, and it is rare to see someone quite so passionate about the construction of a model volcano! Even Juliet would not have been so keen on this experiment. Not only this, but she initially found it difficult to settle in, something that still seems to be the case for myself).

Miss Solomon (Of course, being a Geography teacher, she also adores Geography. Additionally, she is incredibly organised, perhaps even more so than me!).

These three are certainly the *most* similar to me but, after scrutinising the list of every girl in my form, I realise that my character resembles more of my classmates than was perhaps first anticipated.

Melody Luton (we're the only two in our year to wear hair bows to school)

Ally Desmond (she always carries hand sanitiser around with her)

June Pillsbury (we both own and use the Stabilo Swing Cool highlighters)

Beth Parnell (she too attends church every Sunday)

Izzy Vaskin (Neither one of us seems to particularly like ice-cream — I've seen how she picks around it at lunch)

Kimberly —

My pen hovers over the page. Surely there is no way that Kimberly and I have a focal point. Any outsider would assure you that the two of us are as different as can be. I leave an asterisk next to her name, giving myself time for thought.

Despite the fact that she is clearly not an attendee of Lady Nightingale's School for Girls, I add Grandmama to the end of the list on a sticky note.

Grandmama (our relationship seems to be a prime example of the 'nature versus nurture' debate! I doubt that I would be as enthusiastic about reading and learning if it weren't for her. Isn't Mum always saying that I am a miniature version?).

22

Mum drives us to the beach after a lunch of hot lentil soup and garlic bread. The cornish roads are arranged like twine across the fields, twisting so regularly that reading is quite out of the question. Instead I gaze out of the window at the thinning hedgerows, so barren of leaves now that there are large holes poking through the thicket. It is like a collection of sticks gathered for a campfire, arranged carefully into extensive, climbing rows.

BBC Radio Four echoes softly from the car stereo, calming voices filling the vehicle. Without traffic, it's a twelve minute drive to the beach and, given that it is the middle of the day, we arrive correct to the minute. The beach is as empty as the roads: pebbles unmoved and the carpark scattered with only a handful of vans. The nimbus clouds overhead promise rain and I use my closed umbrella as a walking stick as we trek down towards the shore. The coastal winds soar towards us, light but bitter, and we turn our heads. My red-pleated skirt ruffles in the breeze. The pebbles part upon contact with my boot and produce almost as satisfying a sound as the autumn leaves which have littered the field in front of the house. They have formed the most magnificent array of colour — crimson, canary and dijon holding each other tightly in an effort to keep warm. I have taken dozens of photographs from my window, wanting to track this slow and majestic ascent into winter.

The pebble size increases as we migrate towards the seafront, perfectly capturing the process of erosion and, for comparison, I photograph four at different points on the beach. I have changed into my dark green wellington boots so that I can paddle my feet in the ocean. It's a lovely feeling — the water against the rubber. It encloses my feet in a protective bubble which not even Kimberly can pop. My toes are toasty under walking socks and I twiddle them against the waves so that the rubber shifts and presses down at different points. Funnily enough, I actually dislike paddling my feet in the summer. The sandy water sticks to the soles of your feet and rubs against the skin as you walk. In other words, the protective bubble bursts.

We decide to order scones and tea from the café because they've stopped selling ice-creams now for the winter.

"There simply isn't the same demand in this weather," the man behind the counter chuckles. "Hardly a sunny vacation spot in October, is it?"

Whilst we wait, I look around the shop, examining the assorted ornaments, post cards and beach goods. I notice a particularly pretty tea light holder in the shape of a badger and scrape together the necessary £3.50 from my coin purse. I place the candle in the middle of our table — a centrepiece of sorts — as we sip at our warm drinks and listen to the blustering wind as it shakes the clear plastic roofing overhead.

The wind only gets stronger that evening and I once again remind my father how useful it would be to erect a wind turbine in the garden. He bemusedly shakes his head, his gaze still fixed on the television set. I wanted to watch a new documentary on Calvinism this evening and, even though my parents do not necessarily count this as 'entertainment', they dutifully agreed to watch it with me. I massively advocate multitasking and so, instead of just staring aimlessly at the screen, I am knitting. I'm not the best but I suppose that practise makes perfect!

The knitting needles click with the crackling fire and I lean my head on Dad's shoulder. Huddled up under my deep purple dressing gown with a bowl of popcorn at hand, I learn about the spread of Protestantism in North America.

"How many eleven-year-olds would want to watch this?" I hear Dad whisper and my parents chuckle, though not unkindly.

"We're lucky to have her, aren't we?"

***

Seeing as I went to bed an hour early, my alarm sounds at five the next morning. I snuggle up under the covers and read *The Weather Handbook* until six, making notes on a sticky pad as I go along. Ordinarily, I would jot these new factoids into The Book of Knowledge but it's in my desk drawer and I am simply too cosy to rise just yet. My second alarm rings on the hour and I set my book down on the bedside table with a satisfyingly deep breath, planting it neatly on top of my journal. When I was born, Grandmama gave me a simple teddy bear named Camillo and whilst I have decided that I am far too old for toys, I still keep it propped on my bedsheets. I haven't hugged him for years but this morning I hold him tightly to my chest. His fur is still relatively smooth, nothing like the ragged tufts which coat Nathan's own favourite teddy bear, and I nuzzle it against the bottom of my chin.

"I don't want Kimberly to do anything today," I whisper to the bear. "Do you think she will?"

I stare at his misted black pupils and wish that he were Emily, the beautiful doll of Sara Crewe. I always dismissed the notion of animate toys as ludicrous but, in my anxiety, I question myself. Perhaps the bear can hear me. Perhaps, in some queer and irrational way, he can help me. I stare once more at those dull, dark eyes and shake my head sharply. I am much too old for such games.

My hair has gone especially curly overnight and I brush it gently so as to preserve the shape. My hair is principally wavy but, on occasion, large loops arise. I am yet to find out why. I slide in a white alice band and instinctively feel at the tuft of hair at the back of my neck. It has partially grown back and is finally starting to lie flat still manages to upset me and I find tears stinging my eyes. I wipe them away with my thumb and rinse my face in the wash basin. The water is colder than usual and I dab quickly at my cheeks to warm them.

***

On the coach I listen to a podcast about farming in the Seventeenth Century and take a few notes in The Book of Knowledge. The vehicle is so noisy with the sound of chattering children that it's ineffective to read on the way to and from school — I would just end up getting distracted.

I bought my iPod second hand and really only use it for travelling. It holds dozens upon dozens of educational podcasts as well as an array of classical music pieces (though principally Bach). My parents got me the Stephen Fry *Harry Potter and the Philosopher's Stone* audiobook for Christmas last year and I transferred it to the iPod. I much prefer reading, but, in rare and extreme circumstances, it can be very useful. For example, over the summer when driving down a particularly windy road in Spain, reading the text itself was simply out of the question. Finding myself unable to depart from the Wizarding World so suddenly, I could use the audiobook to resume my place.

The coach is much too hot, the heating having been turned up to full, and I take off my blazer to keep cool, the temperature unnatural given the chilly October weather. I gaze out of my window at the amber array of leaves, the colours merging into one another as the bus speeds on. I spot a particularly charming alder tree, its translucent canary foliage almost completely intact. The leaves of the next white oak, however, are so far-gone that I can see through the emptied branches. They intertwine as though fingertips, the spindly twigs crossing over each other in what appears to be a child's pinky promise. There is no overhead skylight but, if there were, I expect I would see an array of yellow, orange and red leaves stuck to the glass.

Someone kicks the back of my chair and I turn around quickly, my hair smacking the side of my face.

"I thought that would get your attention," Ally says. "I was just wondering whether your little injury was feeling any better?"

I nod quickly and turn back around, not entirely prepared for any sort of confrontation this morning.

"It did actually look quite painful," she whispers through the seats. "I don't think Kimberly should have done it".

23

I go to the staff room to ask for Miss Solomon as soon as I arrive at school and my teacher hurries out with a flask of tea, her under-eyes heavy.

"Oh Erimentha. How are you feeling?" she says when she spots me.

I assure her that I have fully recovered and apologise for having been absent from her lesson yesterday. She shakes her head, chuckling slightly.

"You don't have you apologise. It's not your fault you got concussed!"

I nod vaguely.

"I was hoping that you could give me the catch-up work from yesterday? I wouldn't want to fall behind".

"I doubt that you would — we were just reviewing the characteristics of a river. Actually, whilst you're here, I've been meaning to say that I've brought in a book on Globalisation which I think you'll enjoy. I have made a few annotations in the margins — it was one of my university texts, you see — but I'm sure you'll enjoy it nonetheless. You've got ten minutes until registration so why don't we pop up to my classroom now".

I trot dutifully behind her, trying to keep up with her long strides. She's the sort of lady that you would ask for directions: confident in both her thought and action. I used to be like that. I push my chin up to imitate some sense of self-importance.

She finds the book effortlessly and there's a Post-It note on the front: *For Erimentha.*

"Now, don't be put off if you don't understand it. This is tricky stuff but I know how much you like a challenge. I'm happy to go over it with you if you find any passages especially difficult to understand".

She smiles as she hands the book over and I flick through the yellowing pages, smelling the signature vanilla hues of decomposing glue and old paper. It's sweet and warm like a candle that has been left to burn.

"Now you better head along to form. I wouldn't want for you to be late on my accord," she says with a smile and I hurry out of the classroom, thanking her as I leave.

The book is fairly light — only two hundred and fifty three pages — but the first page is, as promised, rather hard to understand. There are at least seven words which I have never before encountered and I note them down in The Book of Reminders during registration. I am so focused on the text that I can't even say whether Kimberly and Izzy are being unkind. I simply don't notice.

"Erimentha, Kimberly and Ally," Mr Aldridge says and I glance up sharply, broken from my intense concentration. I hear a few girls giggle at my reaction.

"Could you meet me in here at short break, please. Ask your teacher whether you can leave their lesson five minutes early. Don't worry though, you're not in trouble, I just need to talk to you three about something important".

***

* * *

144

Mr Aldridge only wants to know what happened in Physical Education the other day and, well, why wouldn't he? He *is* our form tutor after all and I expect that he feels it's his responsibility. We're each asked to recount our version of events but with my deliberately vague answers, Kimberly's lies and Ally's feigned innocence, that doesn't get him very far. He leaves for third period with the same story told on the day: Kimberly lost control of the ball and is *"ever so sorry!"*.

On the way out, she grasps my hand tightly, just as she would a close friend.

"Why don't we all sit together at lunch today? We could talk everything through. Get to the bottom of this little misunderstanding".

I shake my head.

"Sorry Kimberly, I said that I'd eat lunch with your sister actually".

Ally laughs briefly, clearly about to comment on my choice of friends, but Kimberly shoots her a nasty look and smiles sweetly at me.

"No problem. Have fun," she says, before hurrying off down the corridor.

***

As per usual, Ella is in the library. I am hesitant to join her on the armchairs, wondering whether she is mad at me. I haven't seen her since we told her form tutor about the bullying. She is heavily absorbed in her novel and bent so far towards the page that her forehead and fringe do not touch.

"Ella?" I manage.

In the few seconds it takes her to finish her sentence, the butterflies in my stomach exemplify, beating against the epithelial tissue of my stomach. I can feel them gnawing at the gut lining: viciously and ruthlessly. Certainly not as placid as those at the Butterfly Sanctuary we visited last January. When Ella looks up, we will no longer be friends. Her warm eyes will be filled with Kimberly's own hatred and my one chance of a Nightingale friendship will have been swept away by the strong October gales.

I am surprised to instead see a word of thanks on her lips.

"I know I didn't want you to tell but nobody has been mean since you told. Mr Simmons talked to the whole class when I was out of the room and, in our next lesson, everyone was so much nicer to me. Some of the girls even apologised! I know you don't want to tell your teacher, Erimentha, but I don't think you'll regret it. I thought it would only make things worse because everyone would knew that I had told but Mr Simmons said that *he* had noticed it and so I wasn't even called a tattle-tale!"

"Really that's fantastic, Ella! Perhaps you could come round to mine this Friday to celebrate!" I say, avoiding her suggestion.

"I haven't been invited round to someone's house for months!" she says and my heart nearly breaks.

"I can't think why," I say warmly. "You know, you're my best friend, Ella" .

"And your my best friend too", she says, her eyes so large and genuine it makes me want to cry. She returns to her book with a smile planted on her lips.

Surprisingly, the whole day passes without a single incident and I return home with a wider smile than usual. Mum notices and bemusedly asks the occasion.

"Oh, nothing in particular," I say vaguely. "I was actually wondering whether Ella Barton could come round after school on Friday? We've become exceptionally close companions".

"Yes, that sounds like a great idea. But what about Kimberly? You two are in the same year? Won't she be offended?".

"I don't expect she will be. She's probably already got plans. She's got tons of other friends".

Mum agrees half-heartedly and I skip upstairs to make a start on my homework. I've been set three pieces but they take me under an hour to complete (worksheets are remarkably easy tasks, I find!). A clear night sky settles itself above garden s at only 1830 hours and the stars seep through my bay window, regarding the house from their heavenly thrones. It's a still evening and the trees are nearly motionless. It's only occasionally that I hear the 'shh' of the leaves already shed as they trail across the fields. I lie on my rug to make a start on my map of the October night sky, using a silver gel pen to title the black sugar paper. I borrow the family iPad and download a star gazing app to help me name the stars visible from my window. I quickly realise however that this is an outside task. Wanting to look the part, I change into a black star-scattered dress with long velvet sleeves. With my thickest woollen tights and a knitted cardigan on top, I feel toasty as can be.

"Mum, could I just go out onto the patio?" I ask. "I would like to examine the night sky".

"Of course, Bumblebee but please do stay where I can see you — I don't want you getting lost. Oh, and put on a coat, it's rather chilly out there".

I dutifully snuggle up into my duffle coat and slide on some fleece-lined boots, pushing a bobble hat down over my ears. Never having been a fan of stark white torchlight, I use a candle stick to guide me to the outside sitting area. Frustratingly, the light pollution from the house drowns out the sky's freckles, but the app aids me in spotting them. I use a pencil to jot down the positions of the stars and planets, knowing that the gel pen might smudge **without me even realising**. The crisp air is, as Mum predicted, chilly, and despite there being so little wind, I can feel the temperature of my hands dropping. I slip a glove over my left hand and pull down on my hat. My breath is hazy and condenses in the cold, forming a momentary cloud in the otherwise clear night.

24

Once I am finished with the star poster, I check the Book of Reminders and notice the link which Kimberly gave me the day before last. I've been so distracted by the consequences of the tennis ball that I completely forgot to look at the supposed 'Erimentha Parker Fan Club'. I borrow the family computer and type the hyperlink into google, patiently waiting for internet connection. The grey circle twirls round and round like children around a May Pole. Grandmama actually set one up at the Retirement Village a few years ago. I'd loved twirling the yellow ribbon and had dressed authentically for the event, having researched it the day before.

A picture of me pops up on the screen — I have lipstick all over my cheeks and am looking at the camera sternly. My breath falls short and I stare at the photograph blankly as the rest of the page takes form. The photograph forms the header of the website and below there is an introduction for any new internet surfers.

The Erimentha Parker Fan Club
    For all those who can't get enough of Little Miss Pick-Me Parker.

On this website you can find out new facts about Erimentha and her life as well as exclusive pictures that the press don't want you to see!

*"We **love** Erimentha because she is just so cool and popular and smart and we wanted to share this passion with the world" — Fan Club Founder.*

Scroll down to find out some key facts about Erimentha Parker or click on the Gallery to see some photos! xoxox

Following instructions, I drag my finger down the mouse pad.

Facts you didn't know about Erimentha!
1. *Her best friend in the whole world is Miss Solomon, her Geography teacher. We're all so jealous of Miss Solomon! We wish we could spend so much time with Erimentha!!*
2. *She only ever buys clothes in charity shops because she doesn't care about how she looks. Isn't she lucky?!*
3. *She loves experimenting with makeup (as you can see in the photo above, she's a natural!!).*
4. *She once tried to push someone in her class (Izzy) over. She obviously gets angry easily! We don't want to get on her wrong side.*

Next to this, there is a photograph of me which has quite clearly been photoshopped. My eyebrows are crossed, distorting the rest of my face as though the picture has been dipped in water and the ink has run. My eyes have been made a smouldering red and they've even added smoke over the top. This picture could be a mirror because I am indeed fuming. How dare Kimberly do this! Not only is it embarrassing but it must be illegal in some way or another.

Whilst I am not intending on telling on the girls, I screenshot the evidence. I have started a notebook concerning the events of this last month, documenting everything that Kimberly and her friends have done. I keep it hidden at the back of my wardrobe, underneath my summer shoes, where I can ensure that my parents are not going to stumble across it. I click onto the Gallery to see three more photographs — in one of them I have my hand stretched towards the ceiling, my eyes fixed on Mr Aldridge. They have captioned it: *'Once a suck-up, always a suck-up. Don't we just love Little Miss Pick-Me Parker?'*.

I rest my hand lightly on my stomach, feeling rather sick. Kimberly has made her hatred quite clear this term but this website is one step too far. After all, it's public. Anybody could find it. I configure the screenshots on Microsoft Word, printing them quickly whilst Mum is still in the shower. I then clear the internet history, folding up the piece of paper tightly in the palm of my hand.

25

"Kimberly, why did you do that?" I ask in form the next morning. Izzy laughs, rolling her eyes and Kimberly crosses her arms, entirely indifferent to the whole ordeal.

"Do what?"

"Make that website".

"Shouldn't you be happy that someone finally likes you?" she whispers. "This year, not a single kid in our year has been able to suffer your friendship for more than a week. In my class ranking of popularity, you won the bottom place effortlessly. Nobody else even ran close. Isn't it nice to see that you are now *so* incredibly popular? To see that you have your own fan club? Any other girl would be over the moon but you are clearly not grateful for what you have".

She grabs hold of the book that I am holding, her fingernails scratching the hard-back cover. I don't reach for it. I am too focused on her.

"You weren't grateful when we gave you that beautiful haircut. You weren't grateful when I kindly invited you up into my room. And you're not grateful for all the *wonderful* people, like me, around you. We would make great friends, Erimentha. You know that, don't you? It's a shame you had to ruin it for yourself for being so mean and snobby all of the time. You tried to push Izzy over on the first day even though she had done *nothing* to you and were then surprised when we tried to take revenge. You can't expect to act like you do and not be punished, Erimentha. What is it that the Bible says? *Eye for an eye, tooth for a tooth?*"

"But I tell you turn the other cheek," I whisper, so quietly that I doubt it makes a dent in the noise of the classroom. My peers continue with their morning chatter, oblivious to Kimberly's malice. For the first time I understand what Orwell meant when he said that ignorance was bliss.

"And then you have the nerve to come up to me today, all high and mighty, and accuse me of making a website that I didn't even make. You've got real nerve, Parker".

She looks me square in the eye, her irises clearer and brighter than ever. Then she opens the book.

"Property of Miss Solomon," she reads, "So you and your best friend are sharing books now? Oh, how very sweet".

She flicks through the pages delicately. They ripple like pointe shoes tip-toeing across the stage of *The Nutcracker*.

"There are even little notes in it!" she exclaims with insincere gaiety. "Why don't you add some of your own?"

Izzy passes her a pastel green highlighter from my pencil case and Kimberly poises it above the paper. I stand up to retrieve it but Beth pushes me down. The other girls, now distracted from their own conversations, all stare. Many of them are giggling and I can hear *Pick-me Parker* rippling in their whispers.

"It's not my book," I say loudly, trying to hide the tremble in my voice. "It's Miss Solomon's. You can't draw all over it. Not only will she be upset but it's vandalism, Kimberly. You'll get into trouble!"

She looks down on me, almost pityingly and smiles, her mouth pinched and her eyes narrowed.

"But *I'm* not the one who borrowed the book, Erimentha.

153

You are".

She brings down the highlighter and drags it diagonally across the page. Then she does the same to the next page. And the next one. And the next one.

The laughter has become incessant and Beth and Ally are trying to join in, writing silly comments in the margins and ripping the ageing paper of the volume.

"Please stop it!" I whisper, tears streaming down my cheeks. Kimberly is right: it is my fault. I am the one who's going to get into trouble for this. It's just so unfair and this thought only makes the tears stream faster.

"Aw look, ickle Erimentha is crying," Izzy pouts. "What's wrong little one?".

I rub my palms against my eyes, trying to stop the streaming tears, and Kimberly rummages through her schoolbag, withdrawing an orange. She digs her nails into the skin, throwing the peelings my way and looking curiously at the sphere in her palm, as though interested in the vein-like pith. It forms a spider's web over the thin translucent film. She looks up at me briefly and I see a smile pierce the left side of her mouth. She lunges forwards, smashing the orange flesh against my forehead with such vigour that, like a balloon, it bursts. The sticky juice seeps across my face and dribbles drops from my nose and down my chin. The desiccated mass drops into my skirt, leaving a snail-trail in its wake.

"What's the matter? Don't you like oranges?" Izzy asks, barely able to speak, she is laughing so much.

I watch my peers — animalistic and cruel in their response — and it feels like I'm hardly there anymore. Like I'm watching a play at the Globe, or from behind a television show. Some people, like Colton Burpo, have near-death experiences where they detach from their bodies and see themselves from above. And even though, I'm not floating high above the room, I know that I am separate. My mind's

154

substance floats, hardly concerned by what is happening below. I stand up steadily, calm in my revelation, and place the orange in the bin, picking up my satchel and taking the book from Kimberly.

"Kindly tell Mr Aldridge that I am feeling ill and have gone to the nurse," I say, taking my leave with such control that my peers go silent. I think that Beth utters one final remark but I am too forgone to care.

26

True to my word, I do indeed make my way to the nurse, but don't ask to go home. Instead I ask to spend a brief period lying down.

"I still feel a little bit under the weather from Tuesday, I suppose".

Sister Lizzie nods understandingly.

"That was a nasty blow that you took to the head. I'm not surprised you're not feeling your best".

If she still thinks Kimberly hits me on purpose, she doesn't show it.

"If you feel any worse, tell me and I'm happy to phone your Mum and send you home. Do you have a lesson this afternoon that you don't want to miss? Is that why you're hoping to stay in school".

She laughs and I infer that another of the teachers has explained my infatuation with school and learning. I smile along and nod briefly. After all, my intention is to go back to third period. I have English and so only have to see Beth. It's unlikely she'll try anything without Kimberly's tender encouragement.

The infirmary is decorated with children's artwork — half-hearted doodles of flowers and tigers. I notice one by Ella. It's of the seaside with a sun-splattered ocean and one-dimensional seagulls squawking from the heavens. It must be at least two years out of date for the stick figures and clunky colouring are nothing like the doodles she shows me now. She draws her favourite book locations and keeps them as bookmarks. She even made me one of Malory Towers.

***

"I've spoken to Grace and she suggested that Kimberly comes round as well. Apparently she's free and really wants to join in".

Mum looks at me quizzically when I shake my head.

"I really do doubt that she wants to come round," I say, picking at my carrots. "I expect that it's Mrs Barton who suggested it. She probably thinks that it will be some sort of stellar bonding opportunity".

"Wouldn't it though, Erimentha? You two might become really close. I really don't know what's got into you. I won't invite her if you really don't want me to but it does put me in an awkward position, especially since Grace has asked. Do you remember how lovely they were about the barbecue?"

Mum sighs.

"For me?"

I look up at her and find myself agreeing, my stomach tightly clenched and my eyes prickling. I would tell her if I could, but I can't. There is just too much at stake. I try to be optimistic — perhaps Kimberly is trying to make amends? — but the rational side of my brain knows this isn't true.

***

Kimberly hyperbolically declares her excitement the next day, running over to give me a hug in the morning and even gifting a friendship bracelet.

"I'm just so excited for later, Erimentha!" she smiles, baring her teeth. "Everyone's going to be so jealous of our plans! In fact…".

Exercising her self-confidence, Kimberly stands up on a desk and claps her hands to gather the class's attention.

"I'm going round to Erimentha's house after school," she announces. "Try not to be too jealous but she is my new best friend. After all, she's famous, if you haven't already seen her fan club!"

She steps down from the chair and gives my hand a squeeze before launching into excitable chatter. If I didn't know any better, I would think she was being genuine and I find myself rather impressed by her act. Rather than humour her though, I politely excuse myself and turn back to my book, waiting for her to amble back towards her real friends. She taps my shoulder repeatedly, her forefinger heavy, but eventually waves a patronising goodbye.

Kimberly upholds this same level of excitement for the remainder of the day, insisting that we sit together at lunch and even giving me her piece of garlic bread. At break, rather than head straight for the library, I find myself in the thicket of her friends' conversation — an awful discussion all about how ugly June's hairstyle is today. I feel squirm from within their gossiping and their snide comments sting, especially since they are so nice to June's face. I wonder what they say about me behind my back. Making the meagre excuse that I am in need of the lavatory, I bid the girls farewell and Kimberly grips me in a tight hug.

"I'll miss you!" she says, clearly forgetting the fact that a toilet trip is not a month long affair.

I smile weakly.

"I'll wait for you at the end of our mathematics lesson and then we'll head over to the preparatory department to collect

Ella," I say and dart off before further conversation is engaged.

The younger Barton sister is dutifully waiting for me in her favourite armchair when I rush into the library. She has recently started Peter Pan (on my recommendation) and seems to be loving it. I can almost see Neverland and its hostile mermaids swimming under her skull in a sea of wonder.

"I am really looking forward to this evening!" I exclaim, taking the seat beside her. The cushions fold against my weight, easing me into the fabric.

"Me too," she says brightly. "I was thinking that we could even bake some cookies as well. It's definitely the right weather after all".

The rain had been beating against the window panes all day — heavy torrents of water smashing against the glass and obscuring the vibrant greenery of the main field. The wind roars in the perfect October storm, stealing the few golden leaves left on the treetops in its incessant bluster. A part of my wants to go outside but this kind of weather requires thick socks, wellies, jumpers and waterproof coats and my school uniform does not do justice!

27

I have done an extension essay on Poe's 'The Raven' and stay behind after English to hand it in. If I do it during lesson time, my peers can get rather frustrated which only leads to further unkindness. It's easier for everybody this way. In light of Kimberly and my play-date this evening, I doubt that there would have been too much eye-rolling had I handed it in earlier but you can never be too careful. Kimberly waits dutifully, looking surprisingly awkward with one foot holding open the door and her fingers drumming on crossed arms.

"Thanks Erimentha — this is one of my favourite poems. The next one to read is 'The Tell-Tale Heart' but I warn you: it's scary! Check with Mum before you try it".

My reading is rarely regulated by my parents. I am mostly able to judge the suitability of a novel from its reviews. *Frankenstein* and *Dracula* were certainly terrifying but that doesn't mean I must exclude the entirety of the Gothic genre from my reading. Regardless of subject matter, I allow myself to read the Classics, figuring that my literary knowledge is more than limited if I exclude the Canon from my reading list. Me being a massive advocate for rules, I have actually written my own set regarding which books I can and cannot read. I have it laminated and stuck to my bookcase and try to follow it whenever I choose a new novel.

Erimentha Parker's Age Appropriate Reading Regulations:

If more than two swear words are counted within fifty pages each other, the novel is deemed inappropriate. If reading modern adult fiction, the novel should be researched online to see whether language will be an issue. Sexually explicit novels as well as those with an overbearing reference to parties, alcohol and drugs are deemed inappropriate and should not be read. When reading teenage fiction, the age recommendation must be considered and Erimentha Parker cannot exceed an age rating of thirteen. If a biographical novel is inappropriate but the protagonist is a child, the reader can determine whether they would feel happy reading it — after all, if someone the same age has had to suffer through something, it is important that one tries to empathise with them. All Gothic literature is permitted, unless the reader begins to get nightmares, in which case reading of the novel should be terminated. These rules may be overlooked in exceptional circumstances (for example, if the novel has been deemed a masterpiece) in which case, the inappropriate passages must be skipped.

***

Kimberly and I speed walk over to the preparatory department to collect Ella and then meet Mum in the carpark. She has bought us three small packets of dried fruit to share (mango, apple and banana) and I pick happily at the snacks as we each recount our day at school. Even Kimberly laughs along with the conversation, giving a detailed and amusing summary of her lunch break — apparently, Izzy had gone to open the window and accidentally nudged a packet of board pens with her elbow. They'd gone spinning from the window sill and the girls had had to race to retrieve them without getting caught. Kimberly sits the middle seat and Ella gazes up at her with such clear admiration that I try to push away my inhibitions. I don't want to be the one to ruin this evening.

Mum usually works from home but she had a meeting today and the house is chilly. We turn on the heating and I ask whether the other two would like to borrow jumpers, a request which is met with gratitude. Kimberly chooses the green jumper which I wore to her house the other week — the cable knit one which reminds me of pine trees — and she pulls down on the sleeves so that the warm mohair covers her hands.

"I'm so jealous you have a walk-in wardrobe," she says. "I have been begging my parents to get one built but they say I don't need one. Obviously, I disagree. I mean, I've got heaps more clothes than you do".

My wardrobe isn't exactly scarce — I have at least twenty woollen jumpers as well as a dozen dresses — and I wonder how many pieces she owns. I think back to the piles of vestige on her bedroom floor, and that wasn't even including the bits folded in her chest of drawers and wardrobe.

"She really does have a lot," Ella pipes up. "Mummy's always saying that she has more clothes than she'll ever wear. She says that she'll grow out of them before she gets a chance to wear them all".

Kimberly laughs, hiding her face with her forearm.

"Well, *you* have so much stationery!" she says, motioning to the left side of the wardrobe which is neatly packed with everything from protractors to sealing wax.

I agree that I do and look proudly upon my collection. Much of it is from Grandmama. She likes to give Nathan and me little presents — he always gets lego and I always get stationery.

"I like this," Ella says, motioning to a wooden dipping pen. "It's beautiful".

"You can try it out if you'd like? Just bring it over to my desk".

I take out a fresh sheet of faux-parchment paper and a bottle of deep purple ink (I know that this is Ella's favourite colour) and she perches on the desk chair, her tiny legs dangling as she tentatively dips the pen into the ink bottle. The metal nib scratches against the glass at the bottom, but not with enough force to damage it. Her hand is shaking as it hovers over the yellowed paper, thinking about what to write. Mostly, when practising, I simply write my name. It's a principally selfish instinct, I suppose. She sweeps the pen across the parchment, a thick droplet of ink forming when the nib is removed.

"Best friends," I read as she hands the pen back to me.

"Girls, did you say that you wanted to bake cookies?" Mum calls from downstairs. "Do you want to come down so we can get started. I've printed you off a recipe".

I tell her that we'll be down in a second and hurry the pen back to its perch in the wardrobe, leading the way downstairs.

"Hey, Erimentha," Kimberly says. "Where's the toilet? Could I meet you down there?"

I nod and motion to the closest bathroom before skipping downstairs with Ella, the two of us chattering about the Malory Towers series and the difference between Pamela Cox's books and the originals.

The radio is on in the kitchen and 'The Swan' drifts through the speakers, the violin accompaniment squeaking against the wind outside and the piano scrambling up the pantry as we collect the ingredients. It's already growing dark and I light a few of the kitchen candles so that a delightful glow is cast over our workspace.

"We can pretend that we're baking in the kitchens of a Parisian manor in the 19th Century," I suggest, tying an apron around my waist.

"We can both be the servant girls," Ella adds. "Just like Sara and Becky in *A Little Princess*".

"Of course. And cook has left us to make the biscuits for Madam".

"Where's cook then?"

"Because she's meeting with the postman at the tearooms, of course! Don't you remember her saying?"

I am rather a large fan of the early nineteen hundreds and enjoy the game well enough despite supposing myself rather too old. Ella is only nine and I can tell she is enjoying it immensely but I don't know if Kimberly will be the biggest fan when she gets back from the toilet. I look towards the doorway, puzzled. Surely she should be back by now. But I quickly shake these suspicions from my mind. I owe it to Ella to be civil and I don't want to ruin the evening with false accusations.

"Is your Mama the Lady of the House?" she asks.

"Oh but of course".

"And Nathan can be the Lord".

I agree, giggling slightly, as I measure out the coconut oil. Ella, meanwhile, sifts the flour into the mixing bowl, managing to sprinkle the black marble surface white in the process. It speckles the countertop like stars — or a snow flurry on a cold winter's night. Funnily enough, I've always liked the look of spilt flour — there is something strangely calming about it.

"Oh no, I'm to be locked up in the attic again," she exclaims, looking genuinely concerned. "Erimentha, I'm really sorry".

"Don't fear, Mademoiselle. We will clear it up once the recipe has been completed. I am sure that something else will be spilt".

She continues pouring the flour, her nose scrunched up with concentration and her hands steady on the paper bag. Kimberly finally arrives, explaining that she got a little lost on the way down, and, suppressing my suspicions, I greet her warmly. I pass her an apron and ask that she measures out the sugar and dark chocolate chips, a request that she meets with a grin.

Mum puts the cookies in the oven to bake, not wanting us to burn ourselves, and then leaves us to clear up. We have certainly made a mess and the surfaces are coated with flour, sugar and even butter.

Ella offers to wash up, Kimberly dries and I put everything away. We made an efficient team. I bundle the flour and sugar bags into my arms, both packages significantly lighter than they were earlier, and amble over to the pantry. Kimberly follows me with the chocolate chips.

"Did you know that the Mesoamericans used cocoa beans as a currency?" I say as I point her to the chocolate chips' home on the second shelf.

"You sure do like your facts, don't you, Erimentha?" she laughs, closing the pantry door behind her. Her voice is high pitched and forced and quiet enough that you wouldn't be able to hear her from the kitchen. "That's one of the things that I hate most about you."

I turn to face her, surprised more than anything.

"You've been wondering why I dislike you, haven't you?"

Her eyes are cold and blue and clear.

"You think that everyone in the world must *love* you as much as you love yourself and that you are just the most *amazing* person to ever grace the planet. Well guess what, Little Miss Pick-Me Parker, you're not. Nobody in our year likes you".

I shrink back towards the back of the pantry, my shoulders

leaning against the shelving.

"I don't love myself", I try, but she's not listening.

"We wish you'd never come to Nightingale's. You just *had* to come and ruin all of our lives, didn't you? Did you really have to be so selfish?"

"It was my parents' choice," I manage.

"Yeah but you could have changed their minds, couldn't you? If you'd really tried? You know, Erimentha, I'm not going to stop till you get out of our school. Every day will be the same and I can promise you that it will get worse. I *promise* you".

She picks up the bag of flour.

"Stick your hand into it," she says, pushing the packet so close to my face that I feel sick.

Her eyes are hard and I want to cry but, I do as she says and place my palm on top of the soft, white powder, knowing full well that I have now contaminated it.

"Now eat it".

I shake my head, my lips held tightly together and my hair sticking to my wet cheeks.

"I said eat it, Erimentha".

I look at the pile of snow in my palm. My pale skin looks tanned in comparison. There are small craters in the malleable flour which undulate up and down across my palm, seeping into the crevices which some believe tell my future.

Kimberly moves quickly, seizing the flour packet and holding it far above my head. I hold my breath.

"I *hate* you," she whispers with narrow lips.

The flour seems to fall in slow motion, mostly intact as it sails towards my head. I stare at Kimberly — the girl with the pale blue eyes — as it descends. Saint-Saëns's melody drifts from underneath the closed pantry door and I can hear the tap running as Ella washes up the last few bowls.

The flour is so light that I barely feel it hit my head. But I see it. It dissipates, splintering the air like warm breath on a cold day: flailing like smoke from a bonfire on the shoreline. The smoke rises between us, dim under the pantry's single bulb and swimming in rivulets, airy and cold.

The seam of light from the doorway grows as the door is pushed open and the grey cloud fractures before our eyes, pierced by this new-found light. Ella stands in the doorway, her lips parted in immediate understanding.

28

The rest of the evening passes in wistful oblivion. The Barton sisters don't exchange a word and, after showering and sweeping up the mess in the pantry, I suggest that we watch a film. None of us are really concentrating. Kimberly's thumbs are moving furiously across the keypad of her Samsung and Ella's eyes are closed. *Suffragette* is one of my favourite movies and yet I'm too anxious to enjoy it. What is Ella going to do? Everything lies on her shoulders, and we all know it.

My parents don't receive a phone call from Mrs Barton over the weekend and so I can only assume that Ella hasn't said anything. And I'm not surprised. I know that when she opened the pantry door, I lost her friendship — after all, why would she choose me (a girl she's barely known for a month) over her own sister? Knowing that I will no longer have a friend at Lady Nightingale's makes me want to cry, and I found myself more dismal than I have felt all term. Because at least, amongst Kimberly's horridness, I nearly always had a friend to turn to. Now I have nobody.

29

On Monday morning, I rise from bed fifteen minutes after my alarm and force my tangles into a low ponytail so that you can't see where Kimberly cut it last month. I am paler than usual and my eyes are tinged pink. I look ill and, if I asked, Mum would probably let me stay off from school. I shake my head of this thought and check my school bag, leafing through The Book of Reminders for any last minute To Dos. Today I need to hand in my Religious Studies homework and give an updated medical form to the office.

I go straight to the library when I get to school and force a smile when Mrs Athena sees me. It's a bright day and the sun streams through the window, crisp morning light casting leafy shadows across the library carpet. Rather than face Kimberly in the form room, I browse the ethics section of the library, running my fingertips along unbroken spines.

"Erimentha!" Somebody shouts and Mrs Athena utters a gentle 'shh'.

Ella apologises softly and hurries over to me so that she can whisper.

"I've been looking all over for you! I was outside your classroom but you didn't show up. I figured this was the only other place that you could be. Erim, why didn't you tell me that my *sister* was the one bullying you? It makes no sense".

"Because if I did, you'd obviously take her side over mine".

"But that wouldn't be fair — I mean, I obviously love Kimberly best. But I think we both know she was the one in the wrong. I've spoken to her and, well, she says that she's sorry. I really don't know why she was so horrid — especially seeing as I was always talking about you at home — but I do think she actually feels bad", Ella stumbles over her words there are so many. "She said she was angry when she thew the flour and that she wasn't thinking and that she'd never to anything like that again. She wishes she hadn't done it — any of it — now. Honestly, I do understand if you still want to talk to a teacher about this but—".

"No, I don't. Really, Ella. I'd rather this be behind both of us".

Ella embraces me in a tight hug and I can feel her smile on my shoulder. I smile too (because it's impossible not to feel happy when you're with such a good friend!), but my heart also sinks a little. I want to turn the other cheek but it's not fair that Kimberly should make me miserable for weeks and then not get any punishment at all. That we should all just pretend it never happened when it most certainly did. Ella and I plan to read until the registration bell rings, but I just stare at the pages without registering any words. I run everything over in my mind — again and again until it starts to hurt.

In Form, I walk past Kimberly's desk without making eye contact. But her shoulders tense as I pass so I know that she sees me. She only sees my bottom half but it's not too hard to distinguish me: we both know I'm the only one who wears their skirt so long.

"Hey", I hear someone say behind me. "Hey, Pick-Me-Parker? Where're your hundred books? Did Miss Solomon take them back? Did she finally realise how much of a loser —".

"Hey, cut it out Al".

Ally's voice is drowned out by Kimberly's.

"Erimentha's my sister's best friend. She probably lent all those books to Ella".

I know I should turn around and smile. I should be relieved that Kimberly is finally acting nice; that Ella still wants to be my friend. But instead, I just feel entirely empty. Like a felt tip pen which has been used so harshly that all of its ink has been lost.

30

I meet Ella in the library every lunch break and she always meets me desperately.

"How is everything, Erim?", she asks every time. "Is Kimberly better? She's not still being nasty is she?"

She searches my face for upset, but I never let her see it.

"She's a changed person, Ella", I tell her for the fifth time. "She hasn't done anything since last Friday".

Ella's eyes brighten and she squeezes my hand tight, dropping her book to her lap so that she loses her place.

"That's amazing news! Everything just worked out perfectly".

I nod vaguely. I should be over the moon. Kimberly's finally being nice, I've still got Ella as my best friend, and I just got 100% on my English project. But a little something keeps on niggling in my chest. I remember what Pastor John said — about turning the other cheek — but it's so much harder than I ever could have thought. And even though I know she won't try anything, every time I see her turn towards me in the corridor, my heart hammers and I can hardly breathe.

"Ella, just so you know, I promise to you that I will never tell anyone what happened", I say softly. "That I will never get Kimberly into trouble".

Ella squeezes my hand more tightly.

"Thank you, Erim. I don't know how I'll ever repay you".

31

Ella and my pact doesn't last long. I've read that things always come out in the end. That it's part of the natural order of the universe. Mrs Barton found 'The Erimentha Fan Club' on Kimberly's internet history and immediately contacted my parents. When Mum asked me about it, I tried to avoid names but Kimberly's eventually came out into the open.

"I can't believe it" she had said, "and to think that I made you invite her round last Friday. Oh, Bumblebee, I'm so sorry. Why didn't you tell me?"

In answer I had cried — heavy, long, cathartic cries. She'd held me in her arms, her lips against my ear and her warm perfumed cardigan against my nose.

"It's okay darling," she whispered, rubbing my back with warm hands, "It's all over now".

My parents waited until Sunday morning to question me properly. They sat me down at the kitchen table before church, a tray of cinnamon buns in the middle and warm mugs of tea for each of us. Nathan stayed in his bedroom playing lego and the table felt empty without him.

"These are good", mum says.

She smiles at dad, her lips sprinkled with pastry crumbs

and I pick quietly at the crunchy part of the swirl. The kitchen sink tap hasn't been properly fastened and water drips noisily against the white enamel. Mum has turned the radio down but I can just about hear an ad interlude. If they can too, they don't say so.

"Honey, are you okay?" Mum asks after a minute. "I can't believe everything you've had to go through this month. And that you had to go through it all alone".

"I'm okay", I say quietly, my hands placed firmly on my lap and fighting the urge to tap along to the dripping tap water.

"It's okay not to be okay, you know?"

"Your mum's right, Erim. It's totally normal to not feel 100% all of the time. Sometimes I have days where I'm angry, or confused, or helpless. It's okay to feel like that".

"Especially when something bad happens".

"Exactly".

They stare at me intently and I wish that they wouldn't. I wish I was upstairs, or in the library with Ella.

"So are you sure you feel okay?" Mum says. "Because if I were you, I probably wouldn't".

A classical music piece has started playing on the radio — but its so quiet that I can't work out what it is.

"That fan club was terrible", dad says. "I can't believe someone would do something like that".

"Especially Kimberly", mum says softly. "She seems like such a good kid. I really thought you two would be friends".

"And her sister? Is she the same Erim? Has she been causing you trouble?"

I finally look dad in the eye so I can shake my head.

"Ella had nothing to do with it, dad. She's my best friend. When she found out, she actually insisted I tell someone".

"So why didn't you?"

I look back down at my plate and listen to the tap.

"Why didn't you tell either of us, Erim?" mum tries again.

"Because I didn't want to get Kimberly into trouble", I say after a long pause.

"Honey, you must realise that Kimberly *deserved* to get into trouble after making that horrible website".

"I know she did".

"Then why not tell?"

"And why didn't Ella tell her mum? Did she even try talking to Kimberly? Doesn't sound like such a great best friend to me. I know you'd have done that for her, Erim".

"Of course I would. Only Ella didn't know it was Kimberly who was bullying me", I say slowly, only partially telling the truth.

The room goes silent for a second, so that I can hear the classical music piece again. I can hear a string instrument but can't even work out whether it's a cello or a violin.

"And you didn't want to tell Ella because Kimberly's her sister", mum whispers, her voice smiling and cracking at the same time.

I shake my head, tears now rolling down my face.

"And I just wanted it to end. I really wanted them to stop. But I couldn't tell because I didn't want Ella to know".

Mum stands up and hugs me over my chair.

"It's hard to find out that someone you love did something bad", she says into my hair. "But that doesn't mean we shouldn't know. Of course, it would have been hard for Ella to find out. But it's so much harder for you to go to school every day with someone acting like that".

"And remember, it's not even your fault that Kimberly got found out in the end", dad adds with a wink.

"I promise you Ella will still be friends with you, if that's what your worried about".

I bury my head in mum's arm and breathe in her soft, sandalwood scent. Then she wipes my eyes with her finger.

"We're going to go to the school about this tomorrow, Erimentha. Tomorrow morning. It's already booked".

"So we're going to have to know absolutely everything ready for the meeting", dad says.

Forgetting about my cinnamon bun, the tap and the classical music, I finally tell them everything.

***

There is a series of uncomfortably formal meetings at school, some of which I am invited to and some of which I am not.

"Bullying is not tolerated at Lady Nightingale's, Kimberly," Mrs Stafford says. "Surely you know this. And these are very serious accusations — the fan club being only the tip of the iceberg. I have every reason to think that the tennis incident last week was not an accident after all. What have you possibly got to say for yourself, Miss Barton?"

"I'm sorry," Kimberly whispers, her eyes wide.

I have always been taught not to stare and yet I am unable to take my eyes off of Kimberly. Sitting on a chair between each parent, she looks small. Her chin, usually pulled upwards and tilted by an invisible thread, hangs near to her chest and her eyes scan the carpet with nearly as much nervous energy as Simone had on that first day of school. In turn, I look at her shiny dark hair, loose school jumper and pinned back fringe. Then I focus on those eyes. Colourless eyes which had met mine with cold confidence. Eyes whose pale irises I had grown to fear. In the enclosed office of Mrs Allcroft, however, her eyes are darker — perhaps because she's been crying — and, for the first time, I can see Ella in her. I can tell that they are sisters.

"Sorry isn't really good enough at this point", she says sternly. "You made this school a very horrible place for Erimentha. Can you imagine if this had been your first term at this school? How much you would have hated being treated this way".

Kimberly meets my eye but looks away quickly. It's still clear though that her words are meant for me.

"I've never been this sorry".

***

A few meetings in, I eventually, and reluctantly, hand over my log of everything which happened — filed and dated meticulously in my envelope folder. Mrs Stafford says she has never seen anything quite like it.

"My, my Erimentha", she says. "I wish every incident of nastiness at this school was as easy to judge as this. It was very clever of you to keep this file".

I nod sheepishly, still half annoyed that Kimberly is — against mine and Ella's pact not to tell — getting into trouble. But I'm mostly relieved, even though I hate to admit it.

I showed Ella the file before Mrs Stafford.

"I just can't imagine her writing these", she'd said, holding up crumpled notes with shaky hands. "She was just so horrid to you, Erim".

"We don't have to show them if you don't want to, but Mrs Stafford has asked if I have any evidence".

She'd shaken her head slowly.

"Of course you should show them".

I'd hugged her tightly.

"I'm so sorry, Ella".

"No, I'm sorry", she'd whispered back, her eyes watery.

"Bullying of this kind is rarely seen at Lady Nightingale's", Mrs Allcroft, the headmistress, says in one of our final meetings, shaking her head.

"And we appreciate you taking it so seriously", my dad

says.

"Of course we're taking it seriously", she says smiling lightly. "Because this is very serious stuff. The happiness of our pupils is very important to us. Everyone should feel safe at school".

She drums her fingers against the table. The nails are too short to make a sound. Then she he takes off her reading glasses and props them behind her ears, her eyes fixed on mine.

"I've been thinking hard about how we can ensure this will never happen again. How we can make sure that Erimentha never feels unsafe at school again".

My mum leans forwards slightly in her chair. She looks tired and I feel bad for putting her through this.

"In particular, though this is very unusual, I have been thinking about Kimberly's possible expulsion".

My breath freezes in my throat.

"Obviously, we need to make sure Erimentha is happy here. And if that can never be the case with Kimberly in her year, maybe this would be the best option".

Dad nods slowly and Mrs Allcroft focuses on him.

"But obviously this is a huge decision and one I would rather talk through with you both".

I know this question is aimed at my parents. I'm only eleven after all — but I speak before either of them.

"I don't want her to be expelled, Mrs Allcroft".

She leans forward slightly, her elbows propped up on the desk.

"Erimentha, that's very kind of you", she says slowly. "But Kimberly made your life miserable these last few weeks. We need to be sure that she'll never treat you, or anyone else, that way again. Do you understand what I'm saying?"

"Yes, I do understand, Mrs Allcroft. But I still don't want for her to be expelled".

She sighs loudly, her blink lengthened by a fraction of a second.

"And why is that, Erimentha?"

I think back to the image of her little, crouched body in our first meeting. With eyes so wide and red that she looked more like Ella than herself. I think of Kimberly for what she really is — my best friend's sister.

"I don't want her to be expelled because I don't think she'll do it again. Because I think she's truly sorry".

"But how can you know that, Erimentha?"

"She's my best friend's sister, Mrs Allcroft".

"But she was still Ella's sister when she made that website. So, I ask you again, Erimentha. How can you know?"

"I just — I just can".

"I just don't know if you're right, Erimentha".

Mrs Allcroft looks between both of my parents, the office quiet, before telling me to wait outside.

***

Ella comes over on Friday evening. Mrs Barton drops her round and there is tangible tension between our mothers as they say hello. Ella and I curl up on the sofa under thick blankets, the fire crackling and our tongues burning as we sip at hot chocolates.

"Kimberly's not getting expelled", she says after a few quiet minutes. "She's over the moon. Says she doesn't know how to thank you".

I shrug under the heavy quilt and smile softly at her, just happy that Ella is happy.

"But she has to help in the canteen every lunch break for the rest of term. And she's in solitary confinement next week".

"Solitary confinement? Does that mean she won't be in

lessons?"

"It's like being suspended, only you do all of your work in a room at school by yourself".

"It sounds awful".

"But she deserves it", Ella shrugs. "And it's so much better that her getting expelled. You know, she actually really loves Lady Nightingale's".

"I didn't?"

"She was so scared when Mrs Allcroft said she might be expelled. She has loads of friends but she actually finds it hard to make them at first. Like she hates talking to strangers. That's why we never make holiday friends. Because both of us are too shy with new people".

I sip quietly at my hot chocolate, my thoughts hurried and heavy and beating against my skull. I never would have thought Kimberly the type to get anxious about that kind of thing.

"So, as I said, she's over the moon".

The October wind blows against the window panes, and I tuck my knees under the blankets, letting the steam from my mug warm my face. Ella looks at me, her eyes wide and warm and I smile back at my best friend.

32

"Watch out!" Simone shouts, throwing three apples down into the wooden basket.

Ella screams loudly and we crouch to the ground quickly, tucking in our heads so that we don't get hit. Simone laughs from up the ladder, and Melody holds tightly to the bottom so she doesn't fall.

"Hey, that's looks like a good one!" she calls, pointing to one of the higher branches. "Can you reach it?"

Simone is the tallest, which is why we've got her on the ladder. Ella and my arms are so short that we can hardly reach any of the good ones. And Melody hates heights.

We're apple-picking at Honeyed Orchards.

"We picked apples every Fall back home", Simone had explained. "At this place called Apple Annie's. My friends and I loved it. Those apples are just the sweetest you've ever tasted — and even better when you add caramel and sprinkles and coconut. They were absolutely amazing".

I've never been apple-picking but I've heard about it in books and wished I could. And all that time, there had been an orchard just a few minutes away from the Retirement Village.

I apologised to Simone as soon as the whole thing with

Kimberly came out, and she forgave me in a heartbeat.

"I've been bullied too, you know?" she'd said. "For having red hair. People picked on me the whole way through elementary school — said I was a carrot".

"I'm so sorry, Simone. That's horrible. And such a stupid thing to say".

"Isn't it just?! But it's okay. All I'm saying is I get it. Because I was exactly the same. They made me feel so alone that I hardly spoke to anyone in third grade, not even my friends".

Simone's hair hangs down her back in a long braid, shining against the dim autumn sun as she reaches high up the tree and laughs loudly. She throws Melody's apple down gently so it doesn't bruise and Melody grins, declaring it even better in person.

"Ooh and look at how big this one is!" Ella squeals, plucking an especially plump apple from a low branch.

"Now, we should probably save that one for the BFG," I smile.

"Oh I love that book!" Simone says. "You know, I never read any Roald Dahl until I came to the UK".

"I don't know what I would have done without those books when I was younger," I laugh.

"Oh, that reminds me," Ella says, rummaging through her rucksack, "Kimberly asked me to give you this".

She hands me a rectangular shaped parcel wrapped in pink, shimmery wrapping paper. I pick at the sellotape and peel it slowly from the paper so that it doesn't rip. Inside, I find a book, *Wild Magic*, and a note.

Dear Erimentha,

I want you to know that I'm really, really, really sorry for how mean I was to you this term. I don't know why I did it. Mum thinks it's because I was jealous and she's probably right. You're really smart, and actually really nice as well. I am so grateful that you forgive me because I don't think that I deserve that.

I also need to say thank you. I know that I would have been expelled if you hadn't said something. But more than anything, thank you for being such a good friend to Ella. We had no idea that those girls were being so mean to her. She seemed sadder at home but I didn't even think to ask — it shows how good a big sister I've been! I promise that I'm going to look out for her more now and have already told off her bullies myself! Thanks again.

From Kimberly

P.S. You've probably read it but 'Wild Magic' is my favourite book of all time. Ella said that the best present to get you would be a book and so I hope that you like it. I wanted to give you something to show how thankful I am.

***

Back home, I find the list I made after receiving Grandmama's letter — *People who are similar to Erimentha Parker at Lady Nightingale's* — and use a tippex mouse to erase the asterisk. Kimberly and I do indeed share a similarity: we both care about Ella.